"Are you say[ing] marry if you met the right man?"

Maddie laughed. "Now don't go putting words into my mouth, Miles. I'm not a marrying kind of girl."

"So what kind of girl are you?"

* * *

From Here to Paternity—romances that feature fantastic men who *eventually* make fabulous fathers. Some seek paternity, some have it thrust upon them. All will make it—whether they like it or not.

MIRANDA LEE is Australian, living near Sydney. Born and raised in the bush, she was boarding-school educated and briefly pursued a classical music career before moving to Sydney and embracing the world of computers. Happily married, with three daughters, she began writing when family commitments kept her at home. She likes to create stories that are believable, modern, fast-paced and sexy. Her interests include reading meaty sagas, doing word puzzles, gambling and going to the movies.

Look out for Miranda Lee's next riveting romance, A HAUNTING OBSESSION (Harlequin Presents #1893), available in July.

MIRANDA LEE

Maddie's Love-Child

Harlequin Books

TORONTO • NEW YORK • LONDON
AMSTERDAM • PARIS • SYDNEY • HAMBURG
STOCKHOLM • ATHENS • TOKYO • MILAN
MADRID • WARSAW • BUDAPEST • AUCKLAND

ISBN 0-373-11884-8

MADDIE'S LOVE-CHILD

First North American Publication 1997.

Copyright © 1996 by Miranda Lee.

PROLOGUE

'I JUST don't understand you, Miles,' Annabel said in an aggrieved tone.

True, Miles thought. Though to be fair, he didn't understand himself, either. Most men would be more than content with his lot. He seemed to have it all. Money. Position. Power. Not to mention a beautiful and elegant fiancée. A *lady*, no less.

Their wedding was to have taken place in just over four months' time. In June.

But not now.

Miles had broken his engagement to Annabel last night as kindly as he could. He'd had to confess, of course, that he did not love her. It was the truth, after all.

Luckily, the invitations had not yet been sent out, though they had been printed. And Annabel had unfortunately already ordered her wedding gown. He'd offered to compensate her family for any financial loss. He'd also told Annabel to keep the ring—a generous gesture, since it had set him back twenty thousand pounds.

Annabel hadn't quibbled about that, he noticed. Miles didn't think she would. She came from an aristocratic family, complete with mansions and titles, but little cash.

He'd thought the matter had been settled till Annabel had shown up in his office this morning, demanding not further compensation, but further explanation. It seemed she was not going to give up being Mrs. Miles MacMillan lightly.

'Is all this something to do with your father having left control of the family company to Max?' she asked impatiently. 'Is that why you're running off to Australia on the pretext of overseeing the new branch out there instead of taking over the position of vice-president here in London? Because your pride's been hurt by your older brother wielding the whip hand, so to speak?'

Miles's smile was wry as he turned from where he'd been staring blankly out at the rain. What an apt turn of phrase where Max was concerned! His brother did have some peculiar private practices. But no one was supposed to know that. Publicly, he was a perfect English gentleman, complete with stiff upper lip and impeccable manners.

'No, that's not it at all,' he said. 'Max is welcome to the running of the company. Father chose rightly in giving him the job. He's not only better suited, but it's what he's always desperately wanted.'

'And what do *you* desperately want, Miles?' came the caustic question. 'Or don't you desperately want anything?'

An image flashed into his mind—of a woman, a witch of a woman with black hair and black eyes, the palest of skins and the reddest of mouths. Blood red. He could see her now, sashaying towards him across that crowded room, her floaty black dress swirling about her long, long legs, its semitransparent material hiding not an inch of her slender yet sensual curves.

The memory must have projected something into his face, for suddenly Annabel gasped, then glared, her peaches and cream complexion flushing angrily.

'Dear God, it's another woman, isn't it?' She bit the words out. 'You fell in love with some colonial bitch while you were out in Australia on business last year. That's why you've tossed me over, to run back to the arms of some leather-skinned blonde bimbo who probably spends all of her life on Bondi Beach in a bikini!'

Miles was startled by Annabel's viciousness. Plus her capacity for jealousy. Or was it just hurt pride?

There was no doubt Lady Annabel Swanson was one of the most beautiful women he'd ever met. And he'd met a good few in his thirty-three years. Far more beautiful than a certain outrageous creature he hadn't been able to get out of his head, no matter what he'd done.

'That's not so, Annabel,' he said with some of the superb British control his public school education had managed to finally beat into him. 'There is a woman...yes. But I have not fallen in love with her. I'm beginning to doubt I'm capable of falling in love at all,' he said truthfully enough. 'If I was going to fall in love, don't you think I would have fallen in love with you?'

Annabel preened at this, and Miles felt a right hypocrite. More and more he could see her type would never capture his heart, or even retain his desire. She was far too snobbish, far too ambitious and far too mercenary.

As for her performance in bed...she was also far too fond of showers for his liking. He never did relish the feeling that she couldn't wait to wash him from her oh so perfectly painted, powdered and perfumed body. Frankly, he could not bear the thought of touching her ever again.

He simply ached to get away. Yes, to some sun and sand. And yes, into the arms of that witch.

He didn't want to marry her, of course. Heaven forbid. What he wanted was to sink himself deep into her gloriously sexy body, to wallow for a few months in the pleasures of the flesh and not think about England, other people's expectations of him or the infernal family company!

Maybe, after six months, he might be ready to return and get on with the life that had been mapped out for him since birth.

Maybe...

If not, he might do something else, go somewhere else. He had the money to travel indefinitely. His grandmother—his mother's mother—had made him her sole heir. God knows why.

Perhaps because she thought her son-in-law had unfairly favoured his older son. Perhaps because Miles had taken after *her* side of the family and not the MacMillans. She'd been quite delighted, apparently, when she first saw the dimple in Miles's chin, declaring it was identical to her brother Bart's, the black sheep of the family who'd run off to sea and drowned when only a lad.

Who knew what the old lady's reasons had been? She'd died twenty years ago now. Her estate had been put into trust for Miles, and at thirty, he'd become a far wealthier man than Max would ever be. He could afford six *years* in Australia, if that was what he wanted.

Not that he thought he would need that long. A few months' solid bedding of that black-eyed Aussie witch would no doubt cure the unrequited lust that had besieged him ever since meeting her that fateful night twelve months before.

Looking back, he could see that he should have taken her up on her none too subtle invitation. Then maybe his desire for her would not have grown into such an obsession.

But he'd been involved with Annabel at the time and had planned to ask her to marry him on his return to London. His damned sense of honour had stopped him from indulging in a tacky one-night stand, and he'd cut and run before temptation got the better of him.

On coming home, he'd proposed straight away to Annabel, then valiantly tried to forget the way he'd felt in that witch's company. So full of desire and reckless passion. So much a man!

But it had been impossible. In the end, he'd had to face the fact that he did not want to make love to Annabel anymore. He wanted that fiery-eyed witch in his bed, and no one else.

'So it's just sex, is that it?' Annabel snapped.

Miles flashed her an irritated look. 'I've already said I don't love her.'

'Then why on earth didn't you say so earlier?' She heaved an exasperated sigh. 'I'm not a child, Miles. I know what men are like. I have no illusions about their carnal natures. There's not a married woman I know who hasn't had to occasionally turn a blind eye to their husband's disgusting behaviour.

'So you have the hots for this...female. I can understand that. No doubt she appeals to you because she's different from what you're used to. Go to Australia, by all means, and get her out of your system. But when the six months is over, come back, Miles. Come back to me...'

She came forward, the softly understanding smile on her lovely mouth not at all matched by the calculating coldness in her arctic blue eyes. Miles almost shuddered when she put a hand on his arm.

He took a step backwards so that it dropped away. 'I do not want that kind of wife, Annabel. And I do not want that kind of marriage. When and if I marry, I will be faithful. And I will expect the same of my wife!'

'Yes, of course you will,' she cooed. 'But I'm not your wife at the moment, am I? I'm not even your fiancée any more. But I'm still prepared to wait. Don't say no, dearest. Don't dash all my hopes. Let me at least wait till you get back. Then, if you still don't want to marry me, I'll go quietly. I promise.'

Miles made an impatient sound. 'I don't want to give you false hopes, Annabel.'

'I know you don't. You're a dear, dear man, and a proper gentleman through and through. Any other man would have just had this woman on the side and not said a word. I can't tell you how much I admire you, Miles. You're a man of honour. Why do you think I love you as much as I do?'

Miles refrained from mentioning his bank balance.

He was glad when she left, glad to be able to breathe easily again. He'd been half-holding his breath from the moment she'd walked in.

At last he could return to the report he'd received from the private investigator only that morning, barely minutes before Annabel's unexpected arrival. Now he dragged it out of the top drawer and sat down to peruse it at further length.

The quarry had recently broken up with her latest lover, he read again with satisfaction. If she ran true to form, she would not resume the relationship under any circumstances and would not take another man into her bed for several weeks. Though a woman of modern morals, she was, surprisingly, not promiscuous. She rarely had more than one lover a year, and she was always faithful to him.

Miles liked what he read.

He would be presenting himself into her life right at the right time. She'd already showed him she fancied him, so he didn't think he'd have too much trouble becoming her next lover.

His flesh leapt fiercely at the thought. Dear God, he'd never wanted a woman as he wanted Miss Madeline Powers. Never!

Maddie, her friends called her. Darling, she called most men, he'd noticed that night.

He could not wait for her to call him darling.

He could hear the word now, coming low and husky from those scarlet lips. She would whisper it to him as those lush lips travelled over his body, moan it when they fused as one, gasp it every time she came.

Miles could feel his heart hammering away within his chest as he thought of her. He had never met such an overtly sexual creature. She was everything Annabel wasn't. Flamboyant and exotic and wild. She would be hot in bed, he knew. Hot and hedonistic and his!

'Maddie,' he said aloud, and savoured her name. It conjured up images of carnality that would make women like Annabel blanch. 'Maddie,' he repeated, and leant back in his chair, his eyes shutting.

'Maddie...'

CHAPTER ONE

MADDIE'S reaction to Carolyn's baby astounded her.

She hadn't had much to do with babies during her thirty-one years, having always found them annoying, noisy creatures with little to recommend them. They cried incessantly and made the most awful messes from both ends of their restless, wriggling bodies.

But from the moment Carolyn handed over her newborn daughter and she nestled contentedly in her arms, Maddie was enchanted. When the baby's pudgy fingers closed fiercely round one of hers, Maddie's heart had squeezed as tight as the tiny girl's grip. When those unblinking blue eyes looked up at her with total trust, everything inside Maddie just melted.

'Oh, God,' she groaned. 'I never thought this would happen to me, Carolyn, but I think I want one of these for my very own.'

Carolyn laughed softly from where she was propped up against a mountain of pillows in her hospital bed, looking far too lovely, Maddie thought, for a woman who had given birth less than twenty-four hours before. Even the dark smudges under her eyes did nothing to detract from her blonde-haired blue-eyed beauty.

'There's nothing to stop you from having a baby, Maddie,' she said. 'All you have to do is marry Spencer, and Bob's your uncle.'

'Marry *Spencer*? Good Lord, I wouldn't wish that on a dog.'

Carolyn gave her a perplexed look. 'But... but only last month you told me you were crazy about him!'

Maddie grimaced. 'Crazy being the operative word. The man's an insufferable snob. Do you know he started criticising my taste in clothes? He actually said I looked cheap. You don't think Auntie Maddie looks cheap, do you darling?' she crooned at the baby, who seemed entranced by the huge silver hoops that were swinging from Maddie's lobes.

Carolyn decided this was one of those moments when silence was golden. She, personally, would never describe Maddie as cheap-looking. Way out, perhaps. Or off-beat. Definitely Bohemian. Maddie was of an artistic nature. One expected artistes to be different, didn't one?

Carolyn could see, however, that if a man did not really know and love Maddie for the warm, generous and genuine person she was underneath her outwardly outrageous facade, he might mistakenly think her cheap.

Of course, it would help if she dressed differently. Her clothes were always outlandish and her jewellery garish, to say the least. Carolyn wished Maddie would wear a little less makeup and a lot more underwear....

Carolyn's rueful gaze drifted over the outfit her friend was sporting that morning. Skin-tight black leather pants with a matching black leather vest held together with a single wooden button. Every time Maddie moved—or even breathed in—it looked like the precarious closure would pop right open to display her obviously braless state.

'I don't have to get married to have one of these little darlings,' Maddie resumed, glancing up at Carolyn with a minx-like gleam in her flashing black eyes. 'All I need is a suitable sperm donor. He'd have it all, of course. Brains. Beauty. Breeding. I have no intention of introducing an inferior specimen into this poor pathetic world. Someone like this splendid example of human perfection in my arms would be fine.'

She sent Carolyn a wicked smile at this juncture. 'You wouldn't mind lending me Vaughan for a few nights, would you, sweetie? He seems to be one of those prepotent sires who passes on all his good genes.'

Carolyn laughed.

There'd been a time when she'd worried Vaughan and Maddie were lovers. They'd been very close for many years, having been flatmates during their university days, after which they'd gone into business together—Maddie doing the interior decorating of Vaughan's architectural projects.

But despite the intimacy of their ongoing relationship and their relaxed camaraderie, they claimed they had never been physically intimate.

And Carolyn believed them.

Maddie's flamboyant sensuality might have worried a less secure wife, considering the amount of time they spent together. But Carolyn felt supremely confident in her husband's love, as confident as she was of Maddie's friendship.

'You find your own sperm donor, thank you very much,' Carolyn advised with mock tartness. 'And I think I'll have my baby back before your craziness goes off on another tangent and you become a baby stealer.'

'You think I'm joking, don't you?' Maddie smiled as she handed back the tiny bundle. 'About having a baby, I mean, not about wanting to borrow your Vaughan. Much as your hubbie's a gorgeous hunk of male flesh, he's not really my type. Never was.'

'And what *is* your type, Maddie? Spencer?'

'I suppose so,' she agreed happily. 'Lord knows I must be a masochist, but I always seem to be attracted to the sort of supercilious stuck-up silverspoon who wouldn't normally be seen dead with someone like me.'

'And why's that, do you think?' Carolyn asked thoughtfully. 'I mean... I would have thought you'd find such men stifling.'

Maddie shrugged. 'I do, in the end. Especially when they start wanting to change me—or hide me away. That's the kiss of death as far as I'm concerned. Needless to say, dear old Spence got his walking papers the night he decided I would have to change my clothes before he could possibly take me out in public. He rang me every hour of every day for a while, but I simply clicked on my answering machines, both at home and at the office, and in the end, he gave up. Good riddance to bad rubbish, I say.'

Carolyn shook her head, sighing. 'You have a mean streak in you, Maddie. Still, I can't admit to feeling much pity for Spencer. He's a male chauvinist pig, if ever there was one.'

'Then why suggest I marry him, for pity's sake?' Maddie pointed out frustratedly.

'I was only teasing. I knew darned well you wouldn't. You're never going to get married, are you?' Carolyn said, a tender exasperation in her voice.

'No.'

'Is it because of what happened to your mother?'

'You mean do I have some deep-seated Freudian aversion to marriage and commitment because Mama was loved and left by a married man, leaving poor little ol' me behind?'

'Something like that.'

Maddie laughed, tossing her long black curls from her shoulders. She really was a very striking woman, Carolyn thought. And far more complex than anyone realised. In a way, she felt some pity for the pompous Spencer. And any other man Maddie sank her teeth into.

'What a perfectly interesting thought!' Maddie exclaimed, her smile dazzling white behind her lushly scarlet lips. 'It never occurred to me, but you could be right, I suppose. I never try to psychoanalyse myself. I am what I am, and to hell with anyone who doesn't approve of me, which includes Spencer. The last thing I need in my life is some hypocrite of a man who wants to make me over into what he thinks is suitable to his narrow-minded stuffy lifestyle.'

'Good Lord, Maddie! I didn't realise you hated men so much!'

Maddie blinked, startled by her friend's remark. 'But I don't!' she denied. 'I simply *adore* men!'

'Do you, Maddie? Do you really?'

'Of course I do,' she insisted, though not meeting Carolyn's eyes as she looped a stray curl behind her left ear. 'Don't be silly. I can't stand not having a man in my life.'

'Then why don't you want to ever marry one?'

Maddie looked up, deflecting her friend's serious question with a naughty grin. 'Because I like *men*, darling heart, not a single man. I can't think of anything more boring than having to sleep with the same man every night for the rest of my life. Actually, I can't think of anything more boring than marriage in general!'

'Are you saying my life is going to be boring?'

'You and Vaughan are the exceptions to the rule.'

'What about my mother and Julian? They're blissfully happy.'

'Chips off the same block,' Maddie returned, smiling fondly as she thought of Carolyn's still beautiful mother and her husband.

Isabel and Julian.

Such romantic names for such a romantic couple.

Maddie had met them the previous year when Julian, a successful businessman from Sydney, decided to semi-retire on the South Coast and commissioned Vaughan and herself to design, build and furnish a special surprise home for his new bride. Maddie had become good friends with Carolyn when Julian had asked his stepdaughter to oversee the decor while he was overseas on his honeymoon with Isabel. It was during this time that Carolyn and Vaughan fell madly in love, marrying within a few short weeks.

Now, twelve months later, they had this gorgeous little baby.

Maddie leant over and clucked the baby's chin, goo-gooing at it as she'd never goo-gooed before. There was no longer any doubt in her mind. A baby she was going to have. And soon, before the years ticked away and she was too old. She could well afford it, which to Maddie's mind was the only negative against bringing up a baby on her own. What did a child need a father for, anyway? *She'd* never had a father around and she was as happy and normal as could be!

'You're not really going to have a baby out of wedlock, are you?' Carolyn asked worriedly.

Maddie chuckled. 'Trust you to use a term like that! I've never heard anything so old-fashioned in my life!'

'What's old-fashioned?' Vaughan said as he walked in and strode over to the bed. 'Hello, my precious darlings.'

He bent to kiss his wife and baby daughter, the tenderness and love on his face moving Maddie. She'd always known Vaughan was a warm, caring man underneath his outward machismo, but to witness the intensity of his feelings on display for all to see brought a lump to her throat and a tinge of envy to her heart.

'Well?' Vaughan straightened to throw Maddie a questioning glance. 'What's so old-fashioned?'

'Your wife thinks I should be married before I have a baby,' came her dryly amused reply.

Vaughan looked more shocked than in the thirteen years she had known him. 'Good God,' he blurted out. 'You're *pregnant*?'

'No, of course not, you silly man. But seeing your lovely baby girl has sunk a deep well into previously untapped maternal instinct. Yet when I expressed my wish to have a baby, your dear wife insisted I marry Spencer first.'

Vaughan grimaced. 'Good God, not him. Find someone else, for pity's sake. He might be a top solicitor, but he's the most arrogant bastard I've ever met.'

'See?' Maddie pulled a face at Carolyn, who pulled another right back. Both women started to giggle and the baby to cry.

'Here, give her to me,' Vaughan suggested, scooping up his daughter and walking around the room with her, whereupon she immediately stopped crying. 'Speaking of arrogant bastards—' he directed the words at Maddie '—you'll never guess who rang me this morning.'

'If I'd never guess,' Maddie countered, 'then perhaps you should save me the trouble of trying and just tell me.'

'Miles MacMillan,' he announced. 'You probably don't remember him, either of you, but he was at Julian's house-warming party round about this time last year. The night we got engaged, Carolyn. He's British and was out here at the time to plan the opening of a Sydney branch of his family's finance company. Julian was having dealings with him.

'Anyway, apparently he's come back for another six-month stint in Australia and wants to buy a weekender within easy commuting distance of Sydney. Since he'd already seen the South Coast area and liked it, he contacted Julian, who told him about that house I'd nearly finished building at Stanwell Park—the one where the owner went bankrupt, bringing things to a halt. He's driving down to have a look at it this afternoon, and if he likes it, he's going to buy it.'

'I don't remember him at all,' Carolyn admitted. 'There again . . . I did have my mind on other things that night.' And she winked at her husband.

'Wicked woman,' he rebuked, but softly, lovingly.

'I remember him only too well,' Maddie said sharply, and Carolyn and Vaughan's heads whipped round to stare at her.

'No, I did not seduce him,' she added.

Though it wasn't for want of trying. . . .

'But he's not the sort of man one easily forgets,' she went on. 'If one's eyes were not already full of stars, that is.' Her droll tone belied the squirming in her stomach as her mind flashed back to that night.

Miles MacMillan...

Vaughan was right when he called him an arrogant bastard, though Maddie doubted he was a bastard in the literal sense of the word. Not like herself. Miles MacMillan was blue-blooded through and through. If asked, he could undeniably trace his British ancestry right back to the dim dark ages, and there would not be a single entry from the wrong side of the blanket.

None in writing, anyway.

He was upper class through and through. Upper class, upper crust and up himself!

That said, he was also the most maddeningly attractive man Maddie had ever seen. Tall, dark and handsome, with superb bone structure, a squared jawline with a Cary Grant dimple, steely grey eyes and a perversely sensual mouth totally at odds with his coolly controlled air of haughty superiority.

Maddie had found him downright irresistible from the moment she'd spotted him across Julian's living room, standing all alone, dressed in an impossibly stuffy pin-striped suit, not a hair out of place on his dark, well-shaped head, his aristocratically chiselled nose high in the air.

When she'd swanned toward him in her semi-transparent black chiffon dress, he hadn't been able to take his eyes off her. Understandable, considering her seeming lack of underwear—the skin-coloured teddy she was wearing *did* give the illusion of nakedness underneath.

Maddie had foolishly believed he'd been hers for the taking that night, especially once she found out he wasn't married.

How wrong she was!

Oh, yes, he'd been interested, in a sexual sense. She'd been too long on the end of male desire not to recognise the signs. But as much as he'd been aroused by her, he'd also been faintly repelled, she decided later, his ambivalence towards her making him run hot and cold all night. She wondered afterwards if he'd been unable to make up his mind whether to risk his reputation—or perhaps his soul?—by responding to such a shameless creature's advances.

When she'd boldly asked him home for a nightcap, he'd stared at her as though she'd suggested something really depraved. He'd declined politely in a voice reminiscent of Queen Victoria's we-are-not-amused remark, added a curt goodnight, then decamped, leaving Maddie in a most unusual state of hurt, humiliation and anger.

Never before had a male prey of his ilk escaped once she set her sights on him. And never before had a man made her actually *feel* cheap.

But Miles MacMillan had. He'd made her feel lower than the lowest, vilest, slimiest reptile.

Unaccustomed as she was to rejection and humiliation, Maddie had taken some time to get over the incident. Now Miles MacMillan was coming back into her line of fire, and she didn't know if she was excited by that prospect or terrified of it.

Both, she suspected.

'Does Mr. MacMillan know about my business association with you, Vaughan?' she asked archly. 'Does he realise that if he engages your services, he also gets the services of Miss Madeline Powers, interior designer extraordinaire?'

She could not quite recall what she had told their British visitor about herself that night. His cryptic responses had rattled her somewhat. But she rarely prattled on about herself on first meeting with a member of the opposite sex, concentrating on him instead. Presumably he knew nothing about her job, not to mention her passion for painting nude portraits. She usually didn't bring *that* up till the second meeting.

'I haven't mentioned you to him yet,' Vaughan admitted. 'But I doubt there'll be any problem. Wealthy men don't like doing their own decorating, unless they have some female in tow who needs to be pleased. Which there isn't. No wife, fiancée or live-in girlfriend with him. I asked.'

'So our esteemed Mr. MacMillan is still unattached,' Maddie drawled. 'How interesting.'

Carolyn groaned. 'She's off on the prowl again, Vaughan. Do you think you should warn this poor Miles person?'

Vaughan laughed. 'The not-so-poor Miles is well able to take care of himself. If Maddie is silly enough to set her cap at *his* head, then *she's* the one who needs warning. Men like Miles don't lose their heads to any woman. They don't have it in them. They have ice in their veins instead of blood, and computer chips where their hearts should be.'

Carolyn shuddered. 'I don't know what you see in men like that, Maddie.'

'Neither do I,' she returned airily. 'But it's been the same with me as long as I can remember. Still, it's not as though I want to marry any of them. It's strictly on a love 'em and leave 'em basis.'

'Sure is. Once they fall in love with you, you leave them,' Carolyn muttered. 'I hope you're not thinking of soliciting this Miles person to be the father of the baby you've decided you want all of a sudden.'

Surprise sent Maddie's black eyes rounding. The thought had never crossed her mind. But now that Carolyn had mentioned it . . .

Why, Miles MacMillan would be the perfect candidate! Not only did he have the brains, beauty and breeding she was looking for, but he was only staying in the country six months.

No doubt after his exile in the colonies was over, he would wing his way back to merry England, where he would eventually marry some peaches-and-cream-complexioned lady, raise an heir or two in the image of his own stuffy self and end up in *Who's Who* and the House of Lords!

Or was it Commons? No, no, *she* was the one who was common. Spencer had said so the other night, and Spencer would know, the hypocritical creep!

'Vaughan, say something to stop her,' Carolyn said in a panicky voice. 'I can see it written all over her face. She's going to seduce that man. I just know she is!'

'What Maddie does in her private life is her business,' Vaughan pronounced stolidly. 'Besides, you don't honestly think she'd take any notice of me if I tried to stop her, do you?'

Carolyn sighed. 'I suppose not.'

Maddie didn't defend herself, because Vaughan was right. There wasn't a man alive who could stop her from doing what she wanted to do. Men, she'd decided from a very early age, would never play a controlling role in her life. Never!

But seducing Miles MacMillan was more a fantasy at that moment than a reality. Frankly, as perfect a sperm donor as the man might be, Maddie wasn't about to put herself in a position to be humiliated yet again. Rejection was no good for the soul, or her self-esteem.

'Don't worry your pretty little head, Carolyn, love,' she said. 'I do not have my sights set on Miles MacMillan. He didn't want to have anything to do with me last time we met, and I don't want to have anything to do with him now, except in a business sense. So when is his lordship due, Vaughan? Is he coming to the office or are you meeting him on site?'

'He's coming to the office.'

'What time?'

'Around two.'

'Bring him along to meet me then. Best we make sure he's agreeable for me to do his decorating right from the start.'

'You think he might object?'

Maddie shrugged. 'It's on the cards.'

'He damned well wouldn't want to. You're the best interior decorator for miles. I've got no intention of having my perfectly splendid design ruined by a ghastly decor. I'll make it abundantly clear when he arrives that if he wants one of my houses, he gets you, too!'

Maddie smiled and batted her eyelashes at him. 'My champion.'

'I'm not your champion, and you know it. I'm selfish to the core where my work is concerned. Object to you, indeed,' he scorned. 'He won't object when I'm through with him, believe me!'

CHAPTER TWO

MILES didn't know what to make of the situation
or this possible complication. It had never occurred to him that Maddie might be having a thing
with her business colleague. The investigator hadn't
brought up any such possibility, but how else could
one explain Slater's overly protective attitude towards her?

He stared at the man as he pointed out for a
second time that he and Miss Powers were an in-
separable team.

'You buy a Vaughan Slater home, then it comes
decorated by my partner. Take it or leave it!'

The aggressive tone suggested he feared Miles
might not take it, which was ironic. Little did he
know the only reason Miles was buying one of his
damned homes was that Maddie came with it.

Not that the man wasn't a good architect. He
was, if a little unconventional. Miles had thought
Julian's home quite incredible when he'd seen it last
year. Made of steel and concrete and glass, it clung
to a mountainside overlooking Wollongong, giving
it a panoramic view of the city below and the Pacific
Ocean beyond. Miles knew he wouldn't suffer—
either financially or comfort-wise—from buying a
Vaughan Slater home.

'That's fine by me.' It was a huge understatement, delivered quite coolly while he sized up this highly unexpected competition.

Vaughan Slater was a handsome fellow, no doubt about that. And well built, to boot. Around Miles's own six foot three, he had broad shoulders, a strong male face, intense brown eyes and unusual coloured hair. Dark brown mixed with red.

Miles could not imagine Maddie *not* finding the man physically attractive—and vice versa. And the way the man carried on... Well, it was obvious Maddie meant more to him than just a business partner.

Miles hated the idea of their being lovers, but he knew that Slater having a wife and new baby didn't mean he wasn't having something on the side.

Frankly, Miles's view of male morals was even more tarnished and cynical than Annabel's. His father had been an unconscionable rake. His brother was a roué of the worst kind. Most of the married businessmen Miles knew were having dalliances with other women. Hell, just about *all* of them were!

Miles detested that kind of disloyalty. And while he could understand some circumstances where adultery was excusable, he could find none such excuse for the man in front of him. Or Miss Madeline Powers, for that matter.

Slater was married to her supposed best friend, Julian's stepdaughter, Carolyn, a lovely-looking and very nice young woman from what Miles could recall. If Maddie was having an affair with her best friend's husband then he would have none of her. It was as simple as that.

But of course it wasn't as simple as that.

Miles was to realise the extent of his self-delusion as soon as he was escorted along to Maddie's adjoining office.

Slater ushered him past an empty reception area—muttering something about Maddie refusing to have a secretary—then through another door with only the briefest of knocks, catching the woman herself standing at the huge plate-glass window behind her, her back towards them.

For a few distracting moments Miles's gaze was drawn to the breathtaking view of bright blue sky above, turquoise ocean in the distance, crisp white sands closer to hand, then a clean-looking shopping centre directly below. Fifty or so miles to the south of Sydney, Wollongong was one of the most beautiful seaside cities Miles had ever seen.

He took a deep breath, telling himself it was worth it to come halfway across the world for the view alone. But then the witch began turning round, and he knew she alone was the reason for his long journey.

Hell, he thought, as his eyes took in what she was wearing *this* time. Black again. And leather. Tight, tight leather, stretching and straining to encase those long, long legs and that tautly rounded derriere.

The vest top was another story, only a single button holding it provocatively together over obviously braless breasts. Not big breasts. But high and firm and round, the soft, tight leather moulded around them, pressing them together to form a shadowed valley underneath that stupid button.

Miles had never been turned on by black leather before. That was one of Max's kinks.

But he was this time. Or was it the woman within the leather, the witch woman with the tightly curled black hair, which was down today, and fluffed wildly out over her shoulders?

He swallowed and did his best not to look like a man who was dangerously aroused. Suddenly, he knew he should run a mile from this woman. She was going to change his life irrevocably if he became involved with her. He would never be the same again, could never go back to the stolid, staid existence at home. She would sweep him into a world he'd not yet tasted, but which, once savoured, could quickly become an addiction. She was untamed, this creature. Totally wild and tantalisingly wicked.

She would probably corrupt him and was best avoided at all costs.

Miles took a long, hard look at her and wanted her more than ever.

Maddie tried to contain her nerves as she turned round, annoyed with herself for letting a man rattle her. If he looked down his nose at her again, she would not be responsible for her behaviour!

'Vaughan, darling!' she exclaimed, her red lips smiling only briefly before pursing into a reproachful pout. 'You're late again, you bad man. You did say two, didn't you?

'Why, hello, Miles,' she managed airily, making no concession to an ongoing and most uncharacteristic attack of butterflies. 'Long time, no see. Vaughan tells me you're out here for six months and want us to whip up a weekender for you. Is that right?'

His momentary hesitation in answering irritated the death out of her, as did his ongoing and faintly contemptuous survey of her appearance. She used the awkwardly silent moments to do a survey of her own, finding to her disgust that she still thought him the most attractive man she'd ever met. She also realised why she'd been transitorily drawn to Spencer. He was a watered-down version of Miles.

Being faced with the real thing, however, brought home to her the many differences. Miles was taller than Spencer, and leaner and far more elegant. That severely tailored pale grey suit looked superb on him, as did the colour, the same as his eyes. Maddie thought his nose wonderfully patrician, and that dimple in his chin quite irresistible, especially since he always held himself with his chin and nose tilted slightly upwards.

He stood before her, the epitome of beauty, brains and breeding.

He was, no doubt, the ultimate choice for the father of her child. But as such, the ultimate challenge.

For it was obvious from the look on his face that he was still as disapproving of her as he'd been at the party last year. There was no sign, either, of any reluctant desire. His grey gaze remained cold as it swept over her a second time.

He would be a lot harder to seduce than Spencer, Maddie conceded. But all of a sudden, she was determined to succeed. Nothing would stand in her way. It might take time, but then, she had a whole six months. She could afford to take her time, to be a little more subtle than usual, if necessary.

She looked him up and down again and decided he would be well worth waiting for. Ah, but he would make a magnificent donor! With his impeccable breeding, he would surely pass on all those qualities she admired. His looks, his intelligence, his strength, his style.

But none she despised. Because he would not be around to give her child those. His offspring would not learn his snobbishness, or his ruthless ambition, or his cold, callous selfishness. His child would learn nothing but love. He or she would be a true love child in every sense of the word.

'Yes, that's right,' he said at last, his voice as rich and cultured as she remembered. 'I've been assuring Vaughan here that I well understand your services come with purchasing one of his houses.'

I'm counting on it, Miles thought with black irony, having already surrendered himself to the inevitable.

It was some salve to his pride that he would not have to make the running. *She* would do that. Already she was looking him over like a greedy child with a much-desired toy in its sights.

He wondered where *her* pride was. Didn't she have any at all? He'd rejected her advances the last time. Quite brutally. Yet the gleam in her eye suggested she was ready and willing to mount a second assault on his supposed virtue. Lord, if only she knew!

'Have you shown Miles the house at Stanwell Park yet, Vaughan?' she asked, flashing her partner-cum-whatever a dazzling smile. 'If you haven't, then I'll be only too glad to do the honours. That way you can visit Carolyn and the baby again this afternoon.'

'Would you? That'd be great, Maddie. Would you mind, Miles?'

Mind? He couldn't think of anything he'd like better. He wanted her alone. He wanted her anywhere. He just wanted her.

Why, then, did he adopt such a coolly indifferent pose, plus such a formal polite voice? Habit, he supposed. And more of his infernal pride. It was going to be the death of him, that pride.

'If Miss Powers doesn't mind abandoning her work to show me the house,' he pronounced stiffly, 'then I do not object. I would not, however, wish to put her to any inconvenience.'

Maddie resisted the urge to sigh. Instead, she glanced away for a moment. Getting this pompous fool into bed was not going to be easy. Getting him there without protection might prove near nigh impossible! She wondered caustically if his underwear was as starched as his personality. All she could hope was that underneath all that chilling English control lay a real man, with real male hormones.

Looking at him, she caught him off guard for a moment, glimpsing a moment of naked desire in his eyes. It was gone in a flash, but it had been there. She was sure of it.

So! The game was the same as last time. He wanted her yet didn't want her.

It was a game she'd played before, with other men of his ilk. But none, she conceded, of Miles MacMillan's stiff stature and staunch standing.

How good it would be to break that iron control, to have him practically beg her to let him make love to her.

Maddie's eyes narrowed at the prospect. The pleasure of a man's body was nothing compared to the pleasure she gained from his utter surrender to her power as a woman.

Maddie enjoyed sex in her own way but had never had an orgasm in her life. She knew she wasn't capable of it. But she was such a brilliant faker in bed that her lovers never twigged. She always praised their performance afterwards, and they were left smugly thinking they'd satisfied her as well as any man had ever satisfied her.

, Which they had.

Maddie looked at Miles and knew his surrender would give her more pleasure than any man's had ever done. She would not only win the game, but a prize, as well. A baby...

She could hardly wait.

'I'll just get my keys,' she said sweetly, 'and we'll be on our way.'

CHAPTER THREE

MILES clung to the seat belt for added support as the car swung round another sharp curve at far too fast a speed. Lord, the woman drove like a maniac. On top of that, her car was a bomb, an old black thing with a big silver grille in front, which she'd proudly said was one of the original F.J. Holdens, whatever they were.

He wished to God he'd insisted on using his hire car. At least it had air-conditioning. He was beginning to feel rather hot under the collar, not to mention totally frazzled inside.

She was coming on to him again the same as before, with all the subtlety of a steamroller, and he still didn't know how to handle her. It was one thing to think about the sexually charged Miss Madeline Powers from the safety of England, quite another to be faced with the woman in the flesh. Especially when that flesh was poured into black leather.

'Runs like a dream, doesn't it?' she enthused as another curve was successfully negotiated on two wheels.

The road they were traversing generally followed the coastline. It had started out going through sedate village-like streets but had left civilisation behind and was winding a narrow path round the edge of cliff faces. Dangerous drops greeted one to the right, raw mountainside covered in virgin bush rose steeply to the left. The place looked as wild and untamed as the woman next to him.

'Mmm,' was all he could manage.

'Am I driving too fast for you?' she asked in an innocent-sounding voice. 'Just say so if I am.'

He resisted telling her she did everything too fast for his liking. But maybe his pale face gave her the message, for her foot lifted off the accelerator. She laughed as she slowed.

'Vaughan's always telling me I drive too fast. Not that he can talk, the bad man. He has this old red MG with the top down, which he tears around Wollongong in. Though he might have to sell it now the baby's come.'

'You and Slater seem very, er, close,' Miles ventured.

'Oh, we are. *Very*. There's nothing I wouldn't do for Vaughan.'

'Nothing?' Miles echoed in a dryly derisive voice.

Maddie slanted him a look of mock horror, then smiled a devilishly attractive smile. God, but the woman was more than wicked. She was downright irresistible.

'If you're suggesting what I think you're suggesting,' Mr. MacMillan,' she said, 'then shame on you. Vaughan is a married man. Not only that, his wife is my very best friend. Even if I chose to overlook my hard-and-fast rule never to sleep with married men, I could never betray Carolyn. You've met her, haven't you?'

'Briefly.'

'Then you must know anyone who betrayed such a sweetie should have a millstone put around her neck and be cast into the depths of the Pacific Ocean. Anyway, Vaughan's besotted with her. He wouldn't look twice at another woman, and especially not me.'

'Why not you?' he said.

'Because he doesn't fancy me. Never did. We're good friends, nothing more.'

'And you don't fancy him?'

'Heaven's, no. He's not my type at all.'

'And what's your type?'

She gave him a look that made him grateful he wasn't driving. As it was, his heart and loins leapt uncontrollably.

Maddie silently berated herself as she returned her eyes to the road. *You call that subtle, you idiot? You have to play this fellow like a fish. Slowly and very, very carefully.*

But damn it all, she did find him so delicious. She dearly wished to take his startled face and kiss the shock from his mouth and from his eyes. She wanted to whisper wickedly seductive things into his ears and make him squirm with desire, wanted to strip him of those wonderfully stuffy clothes and caress him till he was trembling with need and longing.

An almost alien heat suffused Maddie's whole body at the thought of his flesh fusing with hers. My God, if she didn't know better, she might think she actually wanted this man. In a physical sense, that is.

Impatiently, she dismissed the idea. Impossible! She'd never really wanted a man like that! And probably never would.

This foreign excitement had to have something to do with choosing him as the father of her baby. Knowing that she might conceive made even *thinking* about sleeping with the man so much more marvellously meaningful.

'Is it much farther to the house?' Miles asked abruptly.

'Nope. Fact is, we're here!'

Miles glanced up as the car suddenly zoomed off the road and up a steep driveway, his eyes rounding at the sight of the impressive concrete-and-glass construction looming high over them.

Not dissimilar to Julian's house, it seemed to cling to the cliff, its two storeys sporting identical semicircular balconies, which would give a one-hundred-and-eighty-degree view of the ocean.

The black bomb roared to the crest of the steep slope, levelling out only momentarily before plunging into a large parking area under the building. Miles sucked in a deep breath as Maddie braked to a savage halt barely inches short of the cliff wall at the back of the unfinished garages. The F.J. Holden shuddered as the engine died.

'Sorry about that,' she said without a shred of apology in her voice. 'But I have to give the old girl plenty of gas to get up that drive, then I have to brake hard to stop in time. You won't have any trouble in your Audi.'

'In that case, we'll bring the Audi next time, shall we?' he said, straightening his tie as he struggled out onto still unsteady feet. The tie didn't need straightening. It was just something he did to cover any inner agitation, as though by straightening his clothes he could straighten out his thoughts—and his life. He'd been doing it a lot these past twelve months.

'If you like.' She shrugged indifference to his car as she hopped out from behind the wheel and smoothed down her leather pants.

A thought flashed into his mind of Annabel and her passion for limousines. She wouldn't be seen dead driving around in this old bomb of Maddie's. Or dressed in black leather, for that matter.

Miles knew which woman he preferred and marvelled anew at his apparent lack of taste. His mother would be appalled if she could see him now.

Or would she? he puzzled.

She'd changed since his father's death. Loosened up, for want of a better word. And grown in self-confidence. She'd been surprisingly supportive about his decision to break his engagement to Annabel and take off for far-flung shores for a while.

Miles secretly hoped she would marry again, some nice kind man who would love her to death and dance attendance on her. She deserved it, after his pig of a father. It killed Miles to think he might take after that man in any way at all.

'Anything the matter?' Maddie quizzed him.

Miles blinked, then focused across the bonnet of the car onto her very sexy red mouth. It was wide and lush, and he couldn't wait to be ravaged by it.

'You were scowling,' she added.

'Scowling's a family trait,' he said ruefully.

'Then give it up,' she suggested airily. 'It's unbecoming.'

Miles was taken aback. No woman had dared to criticise him openly in years. He should have chilled any other's woman's temerity with a frosty look. Instead, he found a smile tugging at his mouth.

'All right,' he agreed.

She seemed taken aback for a second before smiling back. 'You know, you're even more good-looking when you smile,' she said with a disarming but charming candour.

Miles might have blushed if his body had known how. 'You think so?'

'I know so. Fact is, Miles MacMillan, you're the most handsome man I've ever met.' Her head cocked on one side, she looked him up and down for the umpteenth time. 'I'd really like to paint you.'

'Paint me? You mean a portrait?'

'Sort of. Painting people is a passion with me. I've been doing it for years and making good money out of it, too. You'd make a perfectly divine subject for my entry in this year's Whitbread Prize. Might I persuade you to sit for me some time?'

'The Whitbread Prize,' he repeated as he wandered round the front of her car to stand less than a metre in front of her. 'What's that?'

'It's an art competition.'

Miles felt hopelessly flattered yet slightly flustered at the same time. It had something to do with the way that glittering black gaze was appraising him, like she was undressing him with her eyes and seeing him without a stitch on.

He cleared his throat uncomfortably, glad his suit jacket was of the new double-breasted style and hid his growing discomfort. 'Wouldn't you be better off with an Australian subject?' he asked abruptly.

'Heavens, no. The subject doesn't have to be known. Frankly, it's better if they're not. Less embarrassing that way.'

Miles swallowed slowly. 'What do you mean? Less embarrassing?'

'Oh, didn't I mention it? All the paintings entered in the Whitbread Prize are nudes.'

'Nudes.' Miles gulped. How could he possibly pose for her in the nude when his body would be raging with desire all the time? Embarrassing was not the word. It would be simply humiliating! 'I, er, don't think I, umm...'

'Don't be silly, Miles,' she interrupted, coming forward to link arms with him and turn him towards the stairwell in the corner. 'I don't do explicit nudes. You won't have to be completely starkers to pose for me. I rarely put faces on my subjects, either. No one will know it's you. Except for me, of course.' Her sidewards smile was erotically suggestive in the extreme.

Frankly, the last thing Miles needed at that moment was anything remotely erotically suggestive. Her arm through his was bad enough to contend with.

She stopped walking and looked at him, her expression expectant. 'So what do you say? Is it a yes?'

He stared into her striking face, with its high, exotic cheekbones, bewitching black eyes and luscious mouth, and knew his answer to her would always be yes. He was hers to command. Only his pride stopped him from openly admitting it, his staunchly embedded British pride.

'We'll see,' came his coolly delivered, almost haughty words. 'Posing for a nude portrait would not be looked upon favourably by the board of MacMillan Credit if it ever got out. I'll have to give the matter some further thought. A man in my position can't just do as he pleases all the time, Maddie. He must always be aware of his reputation.'

CHAPTER FOUR

MADDIE almost laughed at that point. How pompous could you get? But it was rather endearing, in a way. And it would make his eventual seduction all the more satisfying.

'I'll have to know your answer soon,' she said coolly, extracting her arm from his. A tactical retreat at this critical point often worked to splendid effect. 'Otherwise, I'll have to find myself another subject. Entries for the Whitbread Prize close in a couple of months.'

Miles could see his chances of becoming her next lover slowly flying out the window. Why hadn't he simply said yes to posing for the damned picture? Why had he come out with all that guff?

'I'll let you know next time we meet,' he said, still unable to simply say yes.

Maddie sighed expressively and tossed her hair from her shoulders. Both actions drew his gaze— as she knew they would—first to her softly parted lips, and then to where the leather vest strained open for a second as air filled her lungs.

Miles clenched his jaw as his loins leapt once more to attention. The temptation to haul her into his arms and kiss her senseless was acute. Yet he knew he would not be able to stop at kisses, not the way he was feeling.

He glanced around the half-finished area with its dirt floor and rough brick walls. A wheelbarrow stood in one corner, a stack of rough-cut timber in the other. To even *think* about making love in such a setting filled him with self-disgust, more so when the image of taking her in the dirt or up against the wall stirred his flesh to an even fiercer arousal.

As much as his need was reaching monumental proportions, his pride and self-respect remained the stronger forces. He was a gentleman, God damn it, not some wild beast in the jungle. For a gentleman, there was a time and place for everything. And this was not the time or the place.

'You'd better get on with showing me the house,' he said brusquely as he straightened his tie again. 'Time's getting on, and I have to be back in Sydney for dinner tonight.'

It was a lie, but a necessary one. He could not go on like this. He had to get away from her for a while, had to have time to gather his wits and his control. Miles hated anything that smacked of not being in control. It was why he'd fought against her attractions for so long. Even now, having surrendered enough to come in pursuit of her, he still refused to throw all standards to the four winds!

'A business dinner?' she enquired lightly as she led him over to unlock the door to the stairwell.

'Not exactly.'

'You could cancel it, then?'

He threw her a darkly frowning look. 'In favour of what?'

'Since Carolyn's in hospital, I'm cooking Vaughan dinner tonight. The dear man would live on Big Macs if I didn't. I thought you might like to join us. We could use the opportunity to discuss the house. If you decide to buy it, that is.'

A jab of jealousy ripped through Miles. No woman—least of all Annabel—had ever cooked him a cosy dinner at home. Yet Maddie was going to do it for Slater.

Damn it all, he didn't like that one bit!

His resolve to make a quick exit wavered considerably. How could he possibly leave her alone with that hunk? Okay, so they didn't seem to be lovers at the moment, but who knew what might happen? Maddie was obviously feeling the absence of a man in her life, and in her bed. Why else would she have been coming on to him so strongly all day?

Miles had no intention of letting some other man take the place he planned for himself. Only a fool would run off at this point and leave such a wanton creature in such a vulnerable situation. He had no faith in her supposed rule of never sleeping with married men. He suspected most times she simply didn't *ask* if a man was married. She hadn't asked *him* that first night, from what he could recall. The subject had not arisen today, either.

'I'm a very good cook,' she added, her sexy smile intimating she was very good at a lot of things. He didn't doubt it for a moment.

'I think you've just made me an offer I can't refuse,' he pronounced, already fantasising over what he could expect when he became her lover.

Breakfast served to him in bed the morning afterwards, with her still in the nude. Long, lazy summer afternoons spent swimming, and making love, and swimming, and making love...

'Provided I like the house, that is,' he added, his male ego refusing to appear too eager to fall in with her wishes.

He barely looked at the house, giving each room and floor only the most cursory inspection. He didn't really care what it looked like. He was going to say yes to it, as he was going to say yes to the dinner invitation and whatever else was on the menu for afterwards. He hoped like hell *he* was. He hoped he hadn't read the situation wrongly.

'So do you like what you see?' she asked as they stood together on the upper balcony, the one that led off what would be the master bedroom. Miles was pretending to admire the view when all the while he was totally preoccupied with her presence beside him, and the musky perfume wafting from her skin.

'I certainly do,' he said as he turned slowly to face her. Even in the bright sunlight her skin was exquisite, like fine white porcelain. It made her eyes and brows seem blacker than black, her mouth redder than red. Ah, that mouth...

He had to stop looking at it, and thinking about what she might do with it.

'I'll have my solicitor arrange the transfer of deeds as soon as possible,' he stated, then stared at the ocean, his hands curling over the grooved aluminium railing that ran along the top of the balcony wall. Waist height, the concrete wall would eventually be fitted with curved glass windows, which would slide open and closed at the touch of a button.

'That's wonderful!' Maddie exclaimed beside him. 'Vaughan will be thrilled. It's really irked him, not being able to finish it. And I'll have such fun doing the decorating. You *will* give me a free hand, won't you, Miles?'

She reached out to touch him lightly on the wrist. 'You won't be one of those pains of people who wants to tell me how to do my job, will you?'

Miles felt her touch along every nerve in his body. His sidewards glance carried his silent agony as he glared at her long, slender, scarlet-tipped fingers. 'I believe in letting professionals do what they were trained for,' he said stiffly.

'Wise man.' She nodded sagely and let the offending hand drop to her side.

Maddie almost laughed again at this point. Dear heaven, but he was priceless. He took himself and life so darned *seriously*! Not only that, he stiffened up every time she touched him, even casually. Lord, he needed loosening up more than any man she'd ever met. And he needed it soon.

'Will you want me to choose the furniture for you, as well?' she asked, forcing him to look at her again.

She fluttered her long black lashes when he did so and moistened her lips a little with the tip of her tongue. It was reassuring to see that spark of desire still glittering in his eyes as he stared at her mouth. She didn't want him going cold on her. She was looking forward to his eventual surrender far too much.

'The furniture, Miles?' she prompted when he said nothing.

'Oh, er, yes, I suppose so.'

It crossed Maddie's mind that he didn't really care. About the house, or the decorating, or the furniture. Some men were like that. All they wanted was a roof over their head and everything at hand they might need. How it actually looked was of no concern to them.

'I can usually judge what type of furniture my clients will like by simply looking at them,' she ventured. 'Their taste in clothes reflects their taste in most things, I've found. I see you're very conservative and traditional. I'll take that as my cue and go from there.'

'But I don't want a conservative or traditional house!' he surprised her by retorting, quite sharply. 'Or conservative or traditional furniture. Not while I'm here in Australia. I want something different. I want clean lines and plenty of glass and nothing to remind me of England. Nothing fussy. Or dark. Or cluttered. I want a house I can live with. I want a house full of light and air. I want a house that makes me feel alive.'

Maddie could only stare at him, stunned by the passion that had vibrated in his voice as he spoke.

'Blue,' he went on, his normally cool grey eyes blazing with fervour. 'I like blue, and white. Give me blue carpet and white furniture. White walls and glass-topped tables. And a bed big enough to drown in. Other than that, you can choose what you like.'

Her eyebrows lifted in amusement at this last tossed-off concession. 'Well, thank you so much for not telling me how to do my job!' She laughed, her voice carrying both surprise and delight. So he *was* passionate beneath that cool veneer. How wonderful!

He glared at her for a moment, then laughed, too, if a little sheepishly.

'Sorry,' he said. 'I didn't mean to get so carried away. I have no idea where all that came from. I opened my mouth and it all tumbled out.'

'It was your subconscious talking, Miles. People's deepest and truest wishes lie in their subconscious. Maybe you should rely on your subconscious more often. I thought what you said was inspirational. I can see it all now, in my mind's eye, and it's going to be spectacular. What a clever man you are! Come, let's get back to the office, and you can contact your solicitor as well as cancel that dinner you don't really want to go to. There's no time to waste, is there?'

Miles stared into her lovely, vibrant face and thought she was so right. There was no time to waste. None at all.

They turned and walked inside, towards the spiral staircase that would take them to the first floor.

'Afterwards, you can come shopping with me,' she said with infectious enthusiasm as they climbed down the steps, Maddie first, Miles following. 'I have some things I need to buy for tonight's dinner.

I might even let you pick out the wine. Do you like wine, Miles?' she asked when they reached the first floor.

'That depends on the wine.'

She linked arms with him again, and he did not resist her, either physically or mentally. His body and mind raged with lust for her, but alongside the lust was growing a genuine liking. How could you not like such a creature, such a bright, bubbling refreshingly uninhibited creature?

'You'll like Australian wines,' she was saying. 'They're simply marvellous. But watch the Chardonnays. They'll have you under the table before you can say Jack Robinson. There again, perhaps a bottle or two would do you good. You look a little strung out, Miles. Hasn't life been treating you well lately?'

'I've known better years,' he said truthfully.

'But the year's barely begun! I think it's been a perfectly divine year so far. I disposed of the most ghastly man, and Carolyn's had a lovely baby girl. Now you're going to buy Vaughan's white elephant and I'm going to transform it into Shangri-la.'

'Shangri-la?'

'Yes, indeed. I see mystic Eastern influence in the decor you described, and the wish to immerse yourself in your own private and personal paradise.'

'You could be right.'

'Then welcome to paradise, Miles!'

She loved the sound of his chuckle. He was loosening up already. Her eyes gleamed with satisfaction as she smiled at him. *I'm going to make you so happy during this next six months, Miles MacMillan.*

And in return, you're going to make me a mother!

CHAPTER FIVE

MILES could not believe how much he was enjoying himself. Who would have thought he would actually find pleasure in shopping in a supermarket?

It was the company, of course, not the place or what he was doing. Maddie was a highly entertaining person to be with. Intelligent and witty, she constantly amused him with outrageous comments and opinions that would have been severely frowned on in his social circle back home. There wasn't anything safe from her radically feminist viewpoint, especially men.

Reading between the lines, it was perfectly obvious she had a low opinion of the male race in general, if not in particular. Already she'd vented her spleen verbally against three inferior members of the species that afternoon. A male driver who had the gall—plus the stupidity, Miles thought—to pass her on the road. A long-haired lout on a skateboard in the car park who'd made a lewd comment as she walked by. And last but not least, a crabby old man who'd elbowed her rather roughly out of the way in the meat section to grab one of the specials.

'Tell me, Miles,' she said as they wandered down the frozen food aisle, Miles pushing the trolley for

Maddie while she selected the goods. 'What do *you* think of what I'm wearing?'

Miles was immediately on the back foot. Impossible to tell her the truth. No woman ever wanted to know the truth about her clothes, anyway.

'Fantastic,' he said. 'Black suits you.'

'You don't think I look cheap?'

Cheap! It had cost him thousands of pounds to fly out here just to have the privilege of taking all her damned clothes off. How could anything about her possibly be cheap?

'Of course not,' he snorted. 'Don't be ridiculous!'

She slanted him a narrow-eyed glance. 'What about what I wore to that party last year? What did you think of that outfit?'

'Sorry, Maddie,' he lied beautifully. 'I honestly can't remember what you wore that night, other than it was black, too, I think. I'm sure it was very becoming. I do recall thinking at the time what a beautiful woman you were.'

She glared at him for a moment, then laughed. 'What a wonderfully tactful liar you are, Miles. You and I both know I'm not at all beautiful. So... If you were dating me—hypothetically speaking, of course—you wouldn't ever ask me to change my clothes before you took me out, would you?'

'Never!' *I might ask you take the damned things off for a while before I took you out, but change them? Good God, no.* Miles liked her sexy clothes, and her lack of underwear. Her provocative appearance plus her provocative personality were what appealed to him most about her. 'What fool would have done that?' he asked quite truthfully.

'A fool named Spencer,' came her acid reply.

The name rang a bell with Miles. It was the name of her last lover, the one who'd been dumped less than a month ago. Clearly, the fool had tried to turn her into a lady. Who knew? Maybe he'd fallen in love with her and wanted to marry her. Now that was really being a fool. You didn't marry women like Maddie. You made mistresses out of them.

Miles vowed not to make the same mistakes as the recently dispatched Spencer. He had no intention of falling in love with this witch woman. And he wasn't about to try to turn her into a lady, either. God, no! He had a lady at home waiting for him whom he was in no hurry to return to. All he wanted from Maddie was fun—and as much sex as he could handle.

'He does, indeed, sound like a fool,' Miles said dryly. 'You're well rid of him.'

She flashed him a bewitching smile over a packet of frozen corn cobs. 'A man of infinite intelligence! I think I might take you home now and put you to a task more fitting your brain power than wheeling a trolley around.'

He laughed. 'I should warn you. I'm hopeless around a kitchen.'

'I can't imagine you being hopeless at anything, Miles,' she said, almost purring, glancing sidewards at him again from under those long black lashes.

Every red corpuscle in Miles's bloodstream took off at a gallop, charging round his veins at full speed. Hell, the heat she was beginning to generate with her eye contact was downright incendiary. He felt like his body was going up in flames.

'I think I'm all finished here,' she announced with blithe indifference to what she was doing to him. 'A quick visit to the liquor section and we're away.'

Ten minutes later Miles was following her black car out of the car park in his much more comfortable Audi. He'd made her promise not to drive too quickly, as he was unfamiliar with the roads. Only once did he almost lose her when a red light caught him, but she waited for him on the other side of the intersection, and they were soon in tandem once more.

At their relatively sedate speed, Miles had some opportunity to admire his surrounds. The beaches on his right were superb—long and white and clean. He was going to enjoy spending every weekend down here. He was a strong swimmer and didn't think the Australian surf would overly intimidate him. The waves didn't look too high, though that could be misleading from a distance, he accepted. Perhaps once in the water, it would be a different story.

Maddie had, surprisingly, admitted to hating the sun and the sand. Her white skin did not tan, and she spent all summer covered with factor-fifteen sunscreen. Yet she lived right on the beach at a place called Thirroul, which was apparently somewhere between Wallongong and Stanwell Park. They must have passed it twice already that day, but she hadn't pointed it out, and he hadn't noticed any signs.

Miles was beginning to wonder what kind of house an interior decorator who worked for an architect would live in when Maddie turned down a narrow side street on the right. It ran straight toward the beach. A sharp left, however, brought them into another narrow street, which was full of small and rather old cottages.

Miles was surprised when Maddie pulled into the driveway of the third on the right, a white-painted weatherboard cottage with white picket fences, neat lawns and a garden full of flowering shrubs.

He slid the Audi into the kerbside, trying not to compare Maddie's unpretentious but pretty little place with the ivy-clad mausoleum Annabel lived in. Or even his own three-storeyed family home in London, which was as warm and welcoming as an underground railway station.

Again he knew what he preferred.

Any preconception of simplicity and cosiness vanished, however, the moment Miles stepped inside the front door. *My God,* he thought as he followed Maddie into the large living room, which took up the entire left half of the rectangular house.

And the owner of *this* was the woman he'd entrusted with the decoration of his house?

Everything seemed to be black or red, with only a smattering of white thrown in. The ceilings, he noted with some relief, were painted white, but the walls were black, as were the slate floors. Down at

the far end of the room was a large archway leading
into a dining alcove with a square black dining table
and four black leather chairs, with a red Oriental-
style light fitting overhanging the centre of the table.

The closer and larger section of the living room
was dominated by a red rectangular rug around
which were grouped a deep squashy sofa in black
leather and several matching armchairs. A low cir-
cular black coffee table sat in the middle of the rug,
the brass figurine of a greyhound its only or-
nament. There wasn't even the obligatory ashtray.

Miles didn't care. He didn't smoke.

A small black television set crouched unobtrus-
ively on a shelf in one corner of the room, a clean-
lined black bar was built into another, and rows of
clean glasses were lined upside down on shelves
behind it. Two tall brass reading lamps with red
fringed lampshades stood on either end of the sofa.
Several groups of charcoal sketches—all highly
erotic nudes—hung on the walls.

The overall effect was flamboyant and decadent.
Miles was startled, then seduced by the room. His
mouth pulled back into a wry smile. He should have
known Maddie wasn't the white-picket-fence type.

'Great room,' he praised.

She sent him a highly sceptical look, black eyes
dancing. 'I've not long finished refurbishing it. So
tell me, Miles, would you like a room like this in
your house?'

'No. But that doesn't mean I can't like it
in yours.'

She laughed. 'You're just being polite. Still, be assured I don't decorate other people's houses like this. This is for my eyes only, and the eyes of my, er, guests. A man I recently dated told me this room was my inner anger screaming to get out. Silly twit. Would you like to hazard an opinion over my choice of decor, Miles?' she challenged with obviously mischievous intent.

'I think you like black and red,' he said.

She laughed then shook her head at his answer, setting those silver hoop earrings swinging saucily. 'God, but you're so divinely black and white.'

'You think so? I suspect I'm about to embrace shades of grey.'

'Ghastly colour, grey. Except when it's the colour of one particular Englishman's eyes and the superbly cut suit that Englishman is wearing.'

Her black eyes gleamed wickedly as they travelled over him, seemingly stripping him again of his clothes. If his hands hadn't been full of plastic shopping bags Miles might have straightened his tie at that point. As it was, he could do nothing but endure a slash of heat across his cheekbones and another almost painful straining in his loins.

Those grey eyes, which she'd just complimented, flashed with frustration. 'Where do you want me to put these?' he muttered, indicating the shopping bags.

'This way,' she said brightly, and waved him towards an archway that had white saloon-style doors across it. Miles followed with gritted teeth.

You'll get yours, darling, he vowed. *And the sooner the better!*

The galley-style kitchen beyond the swinging doors was both functional and a little less startling than the living room, perhaps because it was black and white, not black and red. Black benchtops, black and white tiled floor, white cupboards and appliances.

'Put the bags on the bench, would you, Miles? Thanks. You're a darling. So what do you think of my kitchen? Better?'

He wanted to stay irritated with her but he just couldn't. 'Now *this* is a kitchen I could live with in my house,' he admitted wryly. 'Though I think I'd prefer navy blue to the black.'

'Done,' she agreed, smiling at him as she started to unpack her purchases. 'Go and have a look at the view from my studio,' she suggested. 'It's through that archway just behind you. It's really just a glassed-in veranda, but the light is good.'

The light was, indeed, excellent, and the view of the ocean superb. The beach started just beyond the back fence, with the water less than fifty yards from where he was standing.

Miles turned from looking at the sea to glance around the studio. The black walls and floor didn't overwhelm here because of the expanse of glass. Down one end sat a bedlike divan with a red velvet throwover and white cushions, down the other stood an easel, with painting equipment spread over a large table next to it. A canvas hung on the easel, but it was covered with a cloth. Miles wondered if it was an unfinished entry for the Whitbread Prize.

Of Spencer, perhaps?

He longed to look at it but dared not be so presumptuous. Instead, he stared out at the sea, which was rougher than it had been earlier, and less welcoming. A sea breeze had whipped up some large waves, which were now crashing onto the shore with a degree of venom.

'Do you ever paint seascapes?' he asked as he walked into the kitchen.

'Tried to a couple of times but I didn't have the knack. No, I stick to what I do best. And what I have no trouble selling.'

'Nudes?'

'That's right. Which reminds me ... you haven't given me an answer yet on whether you're going to sit for me.'

'No, I haven't. I'm still thinking about it.'

'That's okay. Take your time. I'll ask you again later tonight, before you leave. Look, I have to get on with some cooking. Vaughan has a thing for this cheesecake I make, which takes simply ages. Why don't you go watch television or something?'

'Can't I help?'

'I thought you said you were hopeless in the kitchen,' she said teasingly.

'And I thought you said I couldn't possibly be hopeless at anything.'

'Such a memory! I'll have to watch what I say in future. Very well, take off your jacket and tie, roll up your sleeves and I'll put you to work.'

'Finished!' he announced fifteen minutes later, pride and satisfaction in his voice. It was crazy, really, feeling proud of one's vegetable peeling. But he did. It seemed to have more real worth than being a financial whiz-kid. What did he ever see for his foreign exchange deals or clever commodity coups except empty figures on a computer screen? Much better to have a saucepan of expertly peeled potatoes to see for one's endeavours. Much more satisfying all round.

'What do you want me to do next?' he asked eagerly.

She slipped him another one of those looks that curled his toes in his shoes. 'I'd tell you to cut them into chips if I'd ever met a man who could do that bit right,' she said with a wicked gleam in her eyes. 'They always cut them too large and too long. I think it's a phallic-symbol complex.'

'Don't you mean an inferiority complex?' he countered, smiling ruefully. There was nothing remotely inferior about his own phallic symbol at that moment. It had been in a state of intense arousal for so long today he was actually getting used to it. Soon, he would think it was a perfectly natural way to be.

Still, it was some comfort to be standing at the kitchen sink, pressing himself against the steel edge.

'That, too,' she agreed, turning to put the cheesecake in the oven. 'But I'm quite sure you don't.'

'Don't what?'

'Have any complexes at all, let alone inferiority ones.'

'Everyone has complexes, Maddie. Some people are just better at hiding them than others.'

Maddie cocked her head. 'So which ones are you hiding, Miles?'

His expression was one of dry amusement. 'I'll tell you mine if you tell me yours.'

Maddie laughed. Dear heaven, but she was liking this man more and more with each passing second. He wasn't nearly as arrogant as she'd first thought, once you got past his stuffy facade. He even had charm, when he chose to exercise it. And a wonderfully dry sense of humour.

She was going to enjoy being with him much more than she had with Spencer. The feeling of pleasurable anticipation had increased in her all afternoon, much more so than she'd felt with any other man. There was no doubt Miles was special. A special man, she conceded, for a special task—being the father of her baby.

She'd finally worked out how she was going to get him to fulfil this special task without his knowledge and without risk to either of them. If and when he became her lover—and that was still not a foregone conclusion—she would allow him to use protection for a couple of months or so before suggesting they exchange medical clearances, after which she would say she was going on the pill. Maddie doubted he'd object. She'd never known a man who didn't prefer to have sex au naturel, so to speak.

Thinking about Miles becoming her lover brought with it an uncharacteristic impatience. Normally, she didn't mind how long it took to get a man into her bed. In fact, she rather relished dragging out the process of seduction.

But all of a sudden, the thought of Miles leaving her tonight to go to a motel, as he'd said he was going to do, was anathema to her. She wanted him here, in her bed. She wanted to touch his naked body. She wanted to make him want her more than he'd ever wanted any other woman.

She didn't think he'd turn her down this time. If he'd wanted to keep her at a safe distance he would not have come here tonight at all. He'd have scuttled off back to Sydney, as he'd done last year.

Miles was not the easiest man to read, however. Maddie was not nearly as sure of his capitulation as she'd been of Spencer's.

Her heart began to race as she looked over at him. Vaughan would be here soon. If she wished to achieve her aim, the time for subtlety was gone.

'You know, you don't have to go to a motel tonight, Miles,' she said, sounding far more casual than she was feeling. 'You're welcome to stay here tonight.'

Relief crashed through Miles. He'd been worried she might be only teasing him. 'I wouldn't want to put you out,' he hedged, enjoying playing hard to get now that he knew where the land lay. And where *she* would lie. Under him for most of the night, if he could keep it up that long.

'You won't be any trouble,' she said, turning her eyes away from him to start crumbing some slices of meat on a board. 'I always have the guestroom prepared.'

Miles almost smiled. Now who did she think she was kidding? But what the hell? He was happy to play the game her way, as long as he got what he wanted in the end.

'In that case, I accept,' he said. 'What time are you expecting Slater?'

Her nose wrinkled delightfully as she glanced at him. 'Please don't call him that. Call him Vaughan.'

'Very well. What time do you expect Vaughan?'

'I'm not sure. Anytime between now and seven. He knows I always cook for seven-thirty and he likes to have a couple of beers before dinner. Why?'

'Just checking to see if I have enough time for a shower,' Miles told her. A long, cold one, he added ruefully to himself as he looked at his Rolex. 'It's only five past six. I have an overnight bag in the car with a change of clothes in it. Frankly, I'm feeling pretty hot.' Which was the understatement of the year!

'Then go and get it, by all means,' she said. 'I'll be showering and changing myself once I've finished this meat.'

He went to walk past her, but something stopped him. The sight of her tight hard leather-clad bottom, wiggling a little as she worked at crumbing the meat. She immediately looked over her shoulder at him, her hands with their crumb-covered fingers lifting to midair. 'Yes?' she asked.

His eyes rose slowly, stopping at her slightly parted lips, those lips that had tormented him all day. He made no conscious decision to kiss her. He just followed his feelings, taking her chin and turning her slightly to better cover her mouth with his own.

He felt her stiffen with a type of shock when his hand firmly cupped her face, but she didn't stop him by word or deed, so his head completed its downward action and their mouths met.

Was it Maddie who gasped? Or himself? Or both of them?

Miles wasn't sure. All he could be sure of was that her mouth was soft, and sweet, and so full of surrender to his. It seemed to melt into him, her lips falling farther apart under his, inviting a deeper and far more passionate possession.

Miles was loath to accommodate her in that regard, wanting to savour the strange tenderness of the moment for a while longer, to sip at her lips with his, to stroke them at length with his tongue tip before moving on.

'No,' she gasped against his mouth at one point, and his head lifted to gaze questioningly into her dazed-looking face. She was still holding her crumbed hands away from her body, but they looked lifeless and limp. She seemed stunned by his kisses, as though she didn't know what to make of them.

'No?' he echoed, sounding more than a little stunned himself. 'You don't mean that. Surely.'

'No,' she said breathlessly.

He took her second no for assent and reached out to flip open the single button that held her vest together. Her eyes rounded as he parted the leather top and pushed it off her shoulders. It slid down her frozen arms and dropped onto the tiled floor with a plop.

Her breasts were as beautiful as he knew they would be. Small, but perfectly formed and porcelain pale with exotically dusky aureoles and the longest nipples. They invited his mouth rather than his hands, but he wanted to wait for that pleasure. Her breasts weren't going anywhere. He was content to simply touch for now, and watch her reaction. He reached out and stroked gently, teasingly, adoring each desire-swollen breast in turn, each passion-hard peak.

She sucked in one sharp breath after another, her eyes alternatively widening then narrowing. She seemed almost shocked by what he was doing, yet incapable of stopping him.

'Miles,' she moaned at last. 'Oh, Miles...'

He'd never heard his name said like that, with such erotic agony, such impassioned longing.

It blew his mind. He'd never known a woman to become so mindlessly aroused so quickly. He could see what it was that had bewitched dear old Spencer. Women like Maddie were rare. She was a true sensualist, with no artifice or guile. What you saw was what you got.

Miles knew then that what he'd hoped back in England was about to become a reality. He was in for the experience of a lifetime being Maddie's lover, an experience that would be unlike any he'd ever had with a woman. The prospect excited him unbearably.

The telephone ringing startled them both.

'Ignore it,' Miles whispered, refusing to be interrupted at this point. 'Come into the shower with me,' he urged.

She blinked at him through glazed eyes.

The telephone stopped ringing abruptly and an answering machine clicked on, Maddie's voice filling the sudden silence, telling the caller that she could not come to the phone right then—damned right, Miles thought frustratedly—and to leave a message after the beep.

The beep followed, then another younger woman's voice.

'Carolyn here, Maddie. I know you're busy cooking so don't worry about answering. I just wanted to thank you again for giving Vaughan a decent meal and to let you know he's just left, so expect him shortly. He was keen to know what happened with the house at Stanwell Park. I'm sure the news will be good. Just as I'm sure you didn't behave yourself with the handsome Mr. MacMillan. Ring me in the morning and give me all the gory details.'

CHAPTER SIX

THE answering machine clicked off. The silence in the room grew to excruciating proportions.

Maddie could not begin to understand what had just happened to her. Her feelings and responses were totally alien to her past experiences with men. She'd always stayed outside the chemistry of sex before, had acted as a catalyst, promoting passion but not actually participating in it.

To find herself mindlessly turned on by Miles was both amazing and disturbing. She didn't want to feel that way about any man. Yet having felt it, she could not turn her back on those feelings. They were too... exciting.

Her blood was still roaring through her veins, and every nerve ending in her body screamed for more.

She blinked into his eyes, only then appreciating that he was glaring into her flushed face with very real anger.

'I hope Vaughan's wife wasn't implying you're willing to sleep with me in exchange for a contract,' he said in the coldest of voices.

'What?' Maddie was slow to understand what he meant. But once the penny dropped, a bitter resentment went a long way to dampening any lingering desire. How dare he think that of her?

Her blood rapidly cooled, and her outrage was soon joined by embarrassment. Dear heaven, she was actually standing in front of him, naked to the waist!

Maddie had no hang-ups about nudity. Hard to, when her mother had taken her to a nudist camp every summer for years as a child. But she did not fancy Miles seeing the stark evidence of what he'd done to her. Her breasts still felt sensitively swollen and her nipples painfully distended. Snatching her vest from the floor, she dragged it on, her crumbed hands no longer a consideration.

'No, of course she wasn't, Miles,' she said quite sharply. 'Carolyn was referring to my perverse predilection for men such as yourself.'

His anger changed to a startled bewilderment. 'What do you mean, men such as myself?' he demanded. 'And what do you mean, perverse?'

Maddie scooped in a steadying breath. Some disarming was definitely called for, or all would be lost.

'Miles, darling,' she said in a low, sensually charged voice, which she realised ruefully was not entirely put on. 'I've always been attracted to elegantly handsome and successful men with oodles of class, sophistication and style. Why do you think I made a play for you at Carolyn's engagement party last year? There was no contract pending then, was there?

'As for perverse . . . well, that comes from my having little in common with such men, except for the obvious. Hardly the ingredients for a till-death-

do-us-part relationship, which is why I'm still living
by myself, I suppose.'

'Mmm. Are you saying you'd marry if you met
the right man? One you were attracted to and *did*
have things in common with?'

Maddie laughed. 'Now, don't go putting words
in my mouth, Miles darling. Vaughan will tell you
I'm not a marrying kind of girl.'

'So what kind of girl are you?'

'I think you know the answer to that quite well
already. Now go get your overnight bag, and I'll
direct you to the bathroom. Vaughan will be here
soon, and I have to have a quick shower and change
myself.'

'Kiss me first,' he growled, and her heart leapt
with panic. My God, she'd just managed to gain
control of her silly self.

'I don't think . . .'

She yelped when he simply swept her into his
arms and planted his mouth on hers, driving his
tongue deep till she abandoned all hope of resistance. What the heck, she thought. Might as well
lie back and enjoy it.

Amend that to stand up and enjoy it!

Maddie melted into him, her hands snaking
around his neck to press him closer and closer.

When he finally wrenched his mouth away, they
were both breathing hard.

'You're to get rid of Slater as early as possible,'
he ordered. 'Now show me where that bathroom
is, for pity's sake, before I say to hell with your

partner's imminent arrival and throw all decency to the winds.'

Maddie was only too happy to show him where the main bathroom was. Only too happy to escape to her own bedroom with its private en suite while Miles strode out to collect his clothes from the car. For she, too, had been quite prepared to throw decency to the winds with Miles. And how!

It was a staggering thought, and far too new for Maddie to feel totally comfortable with. She needed some time to come to terms with the unexpected person within her Miles evoked with his kisses—this incredibly sensual creature who was a willing prey to his passion, as well as her own, who had no control over her physical responses.

This was an even more staggering thought— Maddie out of control. That was not how the game was supposed to be played. It was the man who was supposed to be out of control, not herself.

It seemed the game was going to be a different one with Miles. Despite some very real concerns, Maddie had to admit it was a game with overwhelming attractions.

How exciting it had been in his arms, with his mouth on hers. How incredibly exciting!

She simply could not turn her back on the pleasure Miles promised.

And what was the harm, provided she did not let Miles realise her response to him was anything new or unusual? No doubt he already believed she was a wild raver, with wall-to-wall ex-lovers. She was only acting exactly as he'd expected her to.

Maddie tried to imagine what making love to Miles would feel like. She could only guess, of course, but her guesses sent a scorching heat raging throughout her whole body.

Groaning, she peeled off her sticky leather clothes and dived into the shower before her temperature went right off the scale. She kept the water hard and cold and the shower brief. Ten minutes later she was answering the door to Vaughan, to all intents and purposes looking and sounding like her usual bright, buoyant self.

'Hello, darling,' she greeted him, giving him a peck on the cheek. 'How's the perfect father of the perfect family?'

'Perfectly nervous about what you're going to tell me. If you say that arrogant fool didn't like my house I'm going to blow a gasket!'

'Oh, ye of little faith!' Maddie replied ruefully as she set off for the kitchen with Vaughan in tow. 'Of course he liked it. And of course he wanted to buy it. Fact is, I made him ring up his solicitor the moment we got back to the office, and the deeds will be transferred by the end of Friday, in less than two days' time. What do you think of that?'

'I think you're fantastic!' he enthused and gave her a hug. 'I also think that calls for a beer, which I will get myself. I wouldn't want to hold up your cooking in any way. I haven't had a decent feed for ages, it seems.'

He strode over to the fridge and was extracting a beer when he stopped and cocked his head, frowning as he listened intently. 'Hey, did you know you'd left your bath running?'

Maddie felt a moment of nerves before deciding not to be so silly. Vaughan was her friend, and as her friend, he had never judged her way of life. 'That's not a bath,' she told him. 'It's a shower. And it's not *my* shower, it's Miles's.'

'Miles's?' Vaughan repeated, a surprised then an exasperated expression zooming into his brown eyes. 'Oh, Maddie, Maddie...' He began shaking his head at her. 'Whatever am I going to do with you?'

She gave him one of her wickedest smiles. 'Absolutely nothing, Vaughan. It's Miles who's going to be doing the honours later tonight, I hope,' she finished with a most uncharacteristic fluttering in her stomach.

Vaughan threw back his head and laughed. 'And I thought you said you weren't interested.'

'Oh, *I* was always interested. I just didn't think *he* was.'

'And you were wrong?'

'Obviously. He's staying the night.'

'Mmm. You're not still harbouring that silly idea about having a baby, are you?'

Maddie bristled. 'It is *not* a silly idea. I'd make a perfectly divine mother.'

'Yes, but Miles MacMillan would not make a perfectly divine father.'

'He won't even know. I don't want his support or his money, Vaughan. All I want is his gorgeous genes!'

'Look, Maddie, I don't particularly care for the man. I think he's a right snob. But I can't condone your tricking him into fatherhood. Frankly, that's not the sort of behaviour I would expect from you. I know you're your own person, but you've always been up-front and honest when it came to men and sex.'

'Is that so?' Maddie countered, feeling quite rattled at being confronted over her past actions with other men and her future actions with Miles. 'Perhaps you don't know me as well as you think you do!'

He stared at her as he popped the beer can open. 'Perhaps I don't.'

'It's really none of your business, anyway. I'll sleep with whomever I please, thank you very much. I've never told you how to conduct your private life.'

'Pigs, you haven't! You're always giving me unwanted advice.'

'Which you never listen to. Keep out of this, Vaughan.'

'All right. But don't say I didn't warn you.'

'As long as you don't warn him,' she answered.

'I won't.'

'You'd better not.'

'Carolyn was right about you. You do have a cruel streak when it comes to men.'

'Only some men, darling. Only some. Now drink up your beer and stop making me nervous.'

Vaughan laughed. 'You don't know the meaning of the word.'

'I didn't once,' she muttered over the cheese-cake. 'But I'm learning.'

'Perverse is a very apt word,' Miles muttered to himself as he stood there, letting the freezing cold water beat down over his body. After five minutes of such self-flagellation, one would have thought his flesh would have shrivelled to less than impressive proportions.

No such luck. It seemed he was going to be besieged by terminal lust till he'd taken that witch to bed for a week or two.

God, but she was everything he'd hoped for and more—an addictive mixture of oddly innocent vulnerability and the most outrageous boldness. A temptress who sometimes seemed strangely untouched. A seductress who acted like *she* was the one being seduced, not the other way around.

It was a lethally arousing combination, which had had him balancing on a knife edge of uncontrollable desire all afternoon. The evening ahead was going to be sheer torture. Miles had no idea how he could endure it.

With class and sophistication and style, he mocked himself. Wasn't that what Maddie said she was attracted to? Hell, if only she knew.

Miles was beginning to suspect that his gentlemanly appearance and demeanour were all a facade. He was a sham, was Miles MacMillan. There was someone else inside his staunchly held British body trying to get out. A wild man. A savage. A beast.

Suddenly, he ached to throw away all the confines of society, to shake his fist at the sort of shallow, snobbish, asinine conventions, which made one do things one didn't want to do and *not* do things one really wanted to do.

It irked him that if it hadn't been for Maddie's lack of convention he would not be here today, feeling more alive—despite his intense frustration—than he ever had before.

In one way, he wished he could be more like her, wished he could discard the gentleman's persona that was becoming more and more a burden to him. But ingrained habits were hard to throw off. As were the rigid upper-class standards that had been ground into him since the year dot.

One of those standards was how one dressed.

Miles stared at himself in the bathroom mirror and shook his head at what he was wearing. In his circles back home, his outfit would be considered smart, yet casual. Navy trousers, a navy and cream striped short-sleeved shirt with navy collar, and cream loafers. He just knew Slater would come dressed in shorts and a simple T-shirt, making Miles feel overdressed and out of place.

As for Maddie... He had no doubt she would change into something equally skimpy. It was hot tonight, and humid. The storm he'd glimpsed brewing out to sea could be some hours away yet.

Miles sighed, then swore. He didn't like to feel at a disadvantage, either with life or with women. Damn it all, he was Miles Henry James MacMillan. Heir to a fortune. Descendant of lords.

Portraits of several of his ancestors hung in some of the great houses of England. How could he *ever* be at a disadvantage?

Miles set his mouth firmly in place while he combed his wet hair straight back from his face, then smoothed the sides washboard flat with his hands. His hair was thick and still had a tendency to wave occasionally if he let it.

Miles never let it.

When he'd been about eight, his father had ridiculed his wavy hair, saying it looked sissy. By the time Miles grew up and realised that his balding father was simply jealous of his son's thick, healthy hair, his hair-grooming habits were fixed. He wore it slicked neatly back from a side part, using gel ruthlessly in his younger years till any wayward waves learned their lesson and only rarely kinked.

One eyebrow lifted at his reflection when he finished.

That's better, Miles, he reassured himself, noting that his mind and his body had settled along with his hair. *You haven't come all this way to have your whole life turned upside down. You've come to eventually put it back on an even keel, to get this witch woman out of your system and then go home, back to your family and your country and your real future.*

You're just living out a fantasy here. Having a fling. Sowing all those wild oats you've been storing up all your life, for fear of ending up like your father. Or your brother.

Miles glanced around the bathroom before he left it. Red and black again, he noted wryly. Yet it didn't look half bad. The guest bedroom, where he'd temporarily deposited his clothes, was totally black and white, with striped checked and geometric designs all over the place. Not a very restful room at all.

He wondered momentarily how Maddie's bedroom would be decorated before quickly brushing the thought aside. Thinking of Maddie in connection with her bedroom was not wise at this juncture. He had himself temporarily under control again, and he wasn't about to lose that control, not till Slater was gone and he had her all to himself.

Then . . . then he would think about beds and bedrooms. Then he would give his mind full reign to the beast lurking within him, and to hell with his control.

CHAPTER SEVEN

SLATER *was* wearing shorts and Maddie not much more, her long, slender form inadequately encased in a swinging little black miniskirt and a black lace blouse that almost gave Miles a heart attack.

Momentarily, he thought she was totally naked beneath it. But what had looked like bare flesh under the semitransparent top turned out to be a skin-coloured lining.

The rest of her was just as provocative. Bare legs. Bare feet. Hair up in a wildly untidy ponytail.

Long red crystal earrings dangled from her lobes, the same dark red as her mouth. She was wearing perfume, too, a muskily exotic scent that would turn on an octogenarian monk.

Slater was perched on one of the kitchen stools when Miles walked in. He stood up and came forward to pump Miles's hand, a seemingly sincere smile on his face.

'So glad to hear you liked the house. I presume you'll want to move in as soon as possible, considering you've only got six months out here.'

'You presume correctly.'

'In that case I can have it finished for you three weeks from next Monday, provided of course that you don't want to change the original plans.'

'Ah, yes...the ones you showed me in your office today. Well, I'm afraid I didn't really absorb them properly at the time.'

Hard to, Miles thought wryly, *when my mind was full of a certain black-haired siren down the corridor.* 'Now that I've seen the real thing I'll be able to transfer the two-dimensional drawings into three dimensions in my mind's eye. I'll drop by your office tomorrow morning and have another look, just in case there might be a small amendment or two. I could also sign a contract with you and Maddie at the same time.'

'Good idea,' Slater pronounced, sounding as pleased as punch.

'Will I be able to actually move in in three weeks?' Miles asked, trying not to sound sceptical. 'Surely Maddie will need more time to complete the decorating.'

Maddie glanced up and tried not to notice how rakishly handsome Miles looked in his more casual clothes.

'I will need at least an extra week before you can actually move in,' she said crisply. 'The painting, light fittings and floor coverings should be completed by that time. And I'll make sure there's enough essential furniture and appliances delivered to make the place livable.

'But I won't compromise on the major pieces of furniture. If what I want is not in stock, I'll have to order. That's where I'm at the whim of others who don't always have total respect for given delivery dates. Still, I've stopped ordering furniture from the worst offenders, so six weeks from next Monday should see everything ready for a house-warming party.'

'That's still impressively quick,' Miles compli-mented them.

'If there's one thing Maddie's not,' Slater said dryly, 'it's slow.'

Maddie flashed her so-called friend a narrowed-eyed glare, and he had the good grace to look apologetic.

'I will do my best, Miles,' she stated firmly, 'but I won't write a definite six weeks' completion date into the contract. And I'll have to opt for longer to cover unforeseen events. Neither will I agree to penalty clauses for non-delivery of furniture if the delay's not my fault.'

'Fair enough,' Miles agreed, giving Maddie a look that carried a degree of surprised respect. Clearly, he'd forgotten she was a professional, with a proper business brain in her head.

Maddie had always had trouble having men re-member that, once their hormones took over their heads. She hoped she wouldn't suffer from the same stupidity herself, now that she had discovered the distractions of real desire. She vowed never to forget what sort of man Miles was. No different to any of the other men of his type she'd become involved with.

Worse, maybe. Being British, he probably had an even more ingrained belief in his own superi-ority than the Australian men she'd dated. Maddie only had to look at his haughtily handsome face and arrogantly regal bearing to be reminded of what she was dealing with.

Unfortunately, every time she *did* look at him, she was besieged with the most undermining sexual feelings that began somewhere deep inside her before rushing to every corner of her body, including her brain.

It was going to be hard to keep her head with this man, she accepted ruefully. But she was determined to, despite everything. She hadn't reached her thirties only to begin making a fool of herself with a member of the opposite sex, no matter what miracles he could perform with that mouth of his! He was going to stay *her* prey, not the other way around.

'Vaughan, would you open one of the bottles of white wine in the fridge and pour Miles and myself a drink?' she asked, her coolly confident voice reflecting her resolve. 'Then take Miles through to the living room and watch the news or something while I cook. I simply can't handle this type of meal and talk at the same time.'

'Will do. Which wine do you want first, the Traminer Reisling or the Chardonnay or the Chablis?'

'Not the Chardonnay,' Miles intervened. 'Maddie tells me that will have me under the table in no time flat. Let's try the Chablis first, shall we?'

'Not me. I'm a beer man, myself. You and Maddie will be drinking the wine.'

'*Three* bottles?' Miles frowned. 'Between just the two of us?' Miles liked a glass or two with meals,

and maybe a port afterwards, but that was all. He'd
been trained to keep a clear head about him during
dinners, since most of these were spent with
business associates or potential clients.

'Sure. Why not?' Vaughan tossed off the question
nonchalantly. 'You don't have to drive anywhere,
and the night's only young. Besides—' he grinned
'—Maddie drinks like a fish.'

Maddie sighed her exasperation. 'Oh, thank you
very much, Vaughan. Now Miles will think I'm a
lush!'

Miles didn't think she was a lush. He thought she
was luscious. And gorgeous. And downright delicious. He didn't want dinner. He didn't want wine.
He simply wanted her.

Instead, he was given a glass of very chilled, very
dry Chablis. Oh, well, he thought resignedly, and
lifted the glass of wine to his equally dry, Maddie-
deprived lips.

Maddie had to congratulate herself on the meal,
despite slightly overcooking the veal. But no one
noticed with the melted cheese and bacon strips on
top. The chips turned out perfect, the green salad
crisp and the passionfruit cheesecake simply
scrumptious.

It was not cordon bleu fare, but Maddie had
always found men like Miles relished simple food
for a change. They spent so much time in res-
taurants and at fancy dinner parties, eating rich
food dripping in creamy sauces, that something like

crumbed veal with chips and salad brought their jaded palates to life.

Next time, she would cook him a big juicy rump steak on her barbecue, complete with her own individually formulated pasta salad. That always went down well.

'I haven't enjoyed a meal so much in ages,' Miles said over coffee, confirming her opinion. 'I must congratulate you, Maddie. You're as good a cook as you said you were.'

'Maddie's a very clever girl,' Vaughan said. 'She can do anything she sets her mind to. Did you know she's a simply brilliant artist as well as an interior decorator? All those black and white sketches on the living room wall are her work.'

'Impressive,' Miles murmured, glancing down the table and locking eyes with her. 'There again, I've been impressed with Maddie from the first moment I saw her.'

Maddie was intensely grateful for the red light overhead. For she could actually feel herself blushing. Which was a first. Maddie never, ever blushed.

'Actually, Maddie's asked me to sit for a portrait,' Miles went on, his eyes never leaving hers. 'What do you think, Vaughan? Do you think I should agree?'

'You do realise she only paints nudes, don't you?'

'Maddie did mention that fact.'

'And you'll probably end up being hung on a public gallery wall as this year's entry in the Whitbread Prize.'

'She mentioned that, as well. Though I was promised I would not be recognisable.'

Vaughan laughed. 'That's what she promised the last chap who agreed to pose for her. Poor fellow's not been able to hold his head up in public since.'

Maddie stifled a giggle, as well, at the memory. The painting had not been an explicit one, but a trick of light on the gallery wall where it had been hung had made a shadowed-in area look like a certain part of the subject's privates.

Unfortunately, it had been an extremely small shadowed-in area.

Still, if the fool hadn't gone around boasting to his male friends about his sexual relationship with her in such a highly exaggerated and not-so-nice fashion, then he wouldn't have had to endure such embarrassment. Maddie had always thought the incident a form of justice for his bragging.

'I think, perhaps, I might pass,' Miles decided.

'I think, perhaps, that would be wise,' Vaughan agreed, smiling.

'And I think, perhaps,' Maddie echoed dryly, 'that most men are cowards.'

Miles arched an eyebrow at her. 'I am not most men. And I am not a coward.'

'Prove it!'

'Don't fall for that one, Miles,' Vaughan warned laughingly.

'I don't intend to. Show me some actual examples of your nudes, and then I will make an informed decision.'

'Vaughan has an excellent one hanging over his bed,' Maddie drawled.

'Oh, no, you don't!' Vaughan protested, as she knew he would. 'No way. He's not bloody well looking at *that* one.'

'Why not?' Miles asked.

Vaughan stood up. '*Because*, that's why. That one's for my eyes only! Look, I'm out of here, or Madam Lash down there will use me as her whipping boy for the rest of the night. I can see she's in a bit of a mood. Maybe you can do something about that, Miles.'

'What do you suggest?'

'Just say yes to whatever she wants, or God knows when your house will get finished. She gets real stroppy when she's not getting her way. See you in the morning, madam. Oh, and you, too, Miles. Don't make it too early, though. I'm bringing Carolyn and the baby home from the hospital tomorrow afternoon, so I'll have to clean up the house before I go to work. Place looks like a whirlwind's hit it!'

Miles didn't say a word while Maddie stood up and escorted her friend, or whatever he was, to the door, then outside to his car. He could hear them laughing together, so it seemed their spat had not been a serious one.

Miles resented, then envied, their easygoing camaraderie. His suspicions over the nature of their relationship had also been resurrected by the mysterious nude hanging above his bed.

He'd never been jealous of a woman before but he was jealous of this one. He didn't care what men she'd been with in the past, but he wasn't about to share her in the present, not with Slater or any other man.

The intensity of his jealousy sent him leaping angrily to his feet, his chair almost crashing to the floor behind him. He righted it, then poured himself another glass of the dreaded Chardonnay, gulping it down as he moved from the dining alcove into the kitchen, then onto the glassed-in veranda. They'd finished the Chablis during the meal, moving on to the Chardonnay during dessert.

It was his third glass, and there was no doubt it was beginning to hit the spot. Miles felt his earlier steely composure giving way to a dangerously untamed aggression. Without a second thought, he strode to the easel in the corner and swept off the dustcover.

The canvas was empty.

He scowled, then looked up to see Maddie standing in the archway, watching him. She didn't look angry. Her face, in fact, was irritatingly unreadable.

'I wanted to see one of your paintings,' he said by way of explanation but without a shred of apology.

'I don't have any here,' she informed him calmly. 'Except for the ones on my walls, and they're only sketches, not proper canvasses. I sell all my nudes as soon as they're done.'

'What of the one your partner has over his bed?' he demanded in sharp tones. 'Did you sell that one, as well? Or did you give it to him as a present—a gift, perhaps, for services rendered?'

Her smug smile infuriated him.

'You have no reason to be jealous of Vaughan,' she said as she undulated slowly towards him. 'I told you... Vaughan is not my lover. He's *never* been my lover.'

She took the empty glass from his suddenly frozen hand and placed it on the table between the paintbrushes, then slipped off her earrings and dropped them in the glass. Miles's heart stopped beating when she turned and slid her arms around his neck, her fingers splaying into his hair.

'Not like you, Miles,' she said softly, her fingertips massaging his skull in the most sensual fashion. 'You're going to be my lover, aren't you?'

'*Aren't* you?' she repeated, her thumbs playing with his earlobes, which were more of an erotic zone than he'd ever imagined.

'You really are a witch,' he said hoarsely, his brain and body becoming oddly disoriented as he blindly surrendered to her will. One part of him was painfully hard, but the rest felt like mush.

'Mmm,' she murmured seductively, then raised herself on tiptoe and encircled his mouth with her tongue tip.

Oh, God. He groaned when it circled his mouth a second time, then stopped. *Do it again, witch,* he urged silently.

When she did his silent bidding a third time, he closed his eyes on a raw moan of mindless arousal. *Do whatever you want with me, witch, only just keep doing it!*

Yet when her tongue suddenly darted between his parted lips, his head jerked back on a startled gasp, his eyes flying open.

Bloody hell! What did he think he was *doing*? He'd never let a woman take control of lovemaking like this before. Never!

And whilst it had a certain perverse appeal, it did not sit at all well with his male ego. No way could he countenance simply lying back while she did whatever she wanted with him.

And that was obviously what she wanted. Not a lover, but a slave. Not a man, but a mouse!

Her history of loving and leaving men took on a clarity he'd not appreciated before. She'd simply got bored with them after a while, bored with their always saying yes to her, bored with their weak-willed, wimpish acceptance of her dominance over them.

Miles did not want Maddie ever getting bored with him. And if anyone was going to be dominant around here, it would be *him*!

A ruthlessly impassioned resolve swept any lingering limpness from Miles's limbs. His hands suddenly gripped her upper arms with a steely strength and he pushed her back to arm's length, his grey eyes glittering with fury and frustration.

'What is it that you think I am?' he challenged angrily. 'Some kind of toy to be played with at your will? I don't know what Australian men are like, but where I come from, it's the man who takes the lead in lovemaking, the man who kisses first, the man who decides when and where and how!'

His surge of testosterone found more than words. He raked his hands down to her wrists and pushed her arms behind her back. Securing them both with a single grip, he reached up with his other hand and took hold of her ponytail, pulling it gently downward till her spine was arched back, her slender white neck offered up to him in attitude of submission.

'No,' came her low moan, the muffled word betraying far more desire than fear. Miles was not fooled. She was enjoying every moment of his masterful treatment. Every single moment.

'Yes,' he growled in black triumph as his head bent to her soft, pale skin. 'Yes,' he muttered again just before his mouth found its mark at the base of her throat.

His satisfaction soared when he felt the throbbing pulse beneath his lips. He sucked hard on her quivering flesh, his mouth grazing a torrid trail up her throat till it covered her ear, breathing hot air into it before he dipped his tongue inside.

The whimpering sounds she made as its wet length filled the spiralled cavern did wicked things to him. God, but he liked hearing her sounds of surrender. He wanted to hear more, wanted her to lose total control under his mouth and hands.

The thought no sooner came into his head than it crystallised into action. He stopped what he was doing to sweep her into his arms, crushing her to his chest in an iron embrace. He left her no room for struggling, no room for anything but useless verbal protests.

Yet she didn't protest, merely stared into his face with widely shocked yet oddly respectful eyes.

Miles had never felt stronger or more of a man than he did at that moment. Her sudden and uncharacteristic subservience filled him with even more desire for this wild creature in his arms and made him all the more determined to master her totally.

It crossed his mind briefly that he was probably drunk, drunk on Chardonnay and frustrated with desire. Surely this couldn't be him treating a woman which such a cavalier, even brutish attitude.

Yet it was. And what's more, he was enjoying it to the hilt.

'Believe me when I tell you.' He growled the words out as he carried her through the house towards his bedroom. 'The only time you'll be on top when I'm in your bed is when I put you there!'

CHAPTER EIGHT

WHITE, Miles saw, and started laughing. She'd decorated her bedroom in white. God, but she did have a sense of humour. Or a wicked sense of irony.

He dumped her across the high brass bed with its lacy white quilt and began stripping off his clothes. When she just lay there staring at him with wide eyes, he had a moment of doubt about what he was doing. But only a moment.

This was no innocent virgin here. She was an experienced woman of the world. A player of very sophisticated games.

What game was she playing now? he wondered. The misunderstood romantic? Nervous bride on her wedding night? Or the captive maiden, about to be ravished by the evil warlord?

Ah, now he rather liked that last one. It suited his own purposes very well.

'You don't have to move,' he drawled, feeling quite dizzy with power. 'Just lie there. I'll undress you when I've finished undressing myself.'

She did just lie there, staring dazedly at him. It might have been unnerving if he'd been capable of being unnerved. As it was, all he could think about was having her naked beneath his equally naked body, having her squirming and squealing with as much frustration as she'd inflicted on him today.

His aim was not to punish, however, but to possess. He was going to overpower her with his passion. He would turn her sexuality against her, use it to enslave her to his needs by making her addicted to her own.

Miles believed he could give her pleasure such as she'd never been given before. Because he was truly mad about her. He would make love to her and make love to her till he dropped, such was the intensity of his desire. And he would not take no for an answer. Too many men, he reasoned, had done so with his virago. She needed to be taught who was boss in the bedroom.

Spurred on by his thoughts, he stepped naked to the side of the bed, reached under her short skirt and yanked her black satin panties down her legs. She gasped.

'I'll get pregnant, you fool!' she cried.

She was the fool, came his savage thought. Did she honestly think that was what he was about to do?

'I doubt it,' he growled, and sank on his knees beside the bed.

She almost jackknifed under him when he leant over her and his mouth found its mark, but he held her still enough to continue quite ruthlessly. Gradually, she stopped struggling, and her choked nos changed to moans of still reluctant but very real desire. When her back started arching from the bed, he smiled a devil's smile against her quivering flesh.

He had her now. There would be no more protests.

And he set about doing everything he knew women genuinely liked, and craved, but were rarely given.

Her abandoned responses thrilled him, as did the way she moaned and moved and finally spasmed, not once but several times. She was as highly sexed a creature as he'd always suspected, still wanting more, pressing herself against him as she writhed and squirmed on the bed.

Miles was amazed how easy it was to control himself when he concentrated on giving her pleasure. But there came a time when he thought it best to stop. He didn't want her totally satiated. Just exquisitely swollen and sensitised.

When he let her go, she moaned her disappointment and her leg fell limply over the edge of the bed. Wanton creature, he thought with dark satisfaction as he stood and stared at her body.

He found the visual picture of her lying there with her skirt pushed up to her waist more of a turn-on than if she'd been totally naked.

Still, the time for visual turn-on was long gone, and he wanted her naked. He placed one knee beside her on the bed and leant over to undo the buttons on her blouse, parting it and staring at her hard-tipped breasts for a few seconds. She watched him with heavy-lidded eyes, clearly unable to move or to say a word.

Miles didn't mind. He was not overly fond of talk at moments like this. Besides, those gloriously erect nipples of hers were beckoning attention from his mouth, and he wasn't about to ignore them any longer.

Gathering her into a sitting position, he peeled the blouse down her arms and tossed it aside before lowering her body to the quilt. She needed some rearousing, he could see, and set his lips and hands upon her breasts with ruthless intent.

Her seemingly startled response surprised him at first. But her softly indrawn breaths soon changed to harsh gasps and moans of naked excitement. He was quite merciless in his ministrations, and was reasonably controlled, once again focusing on *her* pleasure, not his.

But when she splayed fierce fingers into his hair and began holding his head and his lips against her breast in a wildly impassioned fervour, Miles finally began to lose control. His mouth turned savage, the beast rising within him. He nipped as well as sucked, his hands not at all gentle on her other breast.

She cried out. And whilst he did wrench his mouth away from the tortured peak, it was only to take savage possession of her mouth instead. His legs pried hers apart as he kissed her, his body looming tense and large over her as he positioned himself for mating with her. Every animal instinct was goading him to simply plunge into her ready flesh, to drive deep and hard, to lose himself completely in the primitive pleasure of the moment.

He almost didn't stop. For a split second, their immediate future hung in the balance, but then common sense returned, and with it a degree of frustration. Why did he always have to be so damned sensible?

'Won't be long,' he muttered and forced himself off the bed before he could change his mind.

He'd come well prepared for safe sex, but he fumbled through the wrong pockets for ages before finally locating one of the condoms he'd brought with him. He sat on the side of the bed, his back to her, as he did what he had to do, his hands shaking as they'd never shook before.

'Miles ...'

'What?' he snapped, irritated with himself and the situation. When he glanced over his shoulder, he was surprised to see she had moved and was lying properly on the bed, with her head on the pillow. She'd pulled her hair out of the ponytail as well, and her black curls were spread out on the white pillow.

She looked beautiful, he thought, and yes ... oddly innocent, despite her bruised mouth and wildly glittering eyes.

She rolled on her side and smiled softly at him. And then she did something that really shocked him. She held out her arms, and a look of real love filled her face.

Miles groaned. How could he resist? She was offering him a haven such as he'd never known. Or so it seemed.

He found himself crawling over the bed and into her arms. Her mouth was sweet, her legs like silk as they wrapped high around him. And then his flesh was filling hers, and he was flying, flying high above the clouds, high above the cold, cruel world to a land where nothing existed but the exquisite heat of her woman's body and the sounds of her soft cries in his ears.

It was only afterwards, when he'd come back to earth, that he tried to make sense of the experience.

He lay on top of her, his heart still pounding, his head still whirling.

There'd been more to it than sex, surely. It had been an oddly out-of-body experience, an emotional as well as a physical bonding. A making love, he finally accepted, not just the sating of desire.

Or it had been for him.

Finally, he levered himself from her slender form and stared into her face. But her eyes were shut, and she was breathing the slow heavy breathing of a contented sleeper. No tortured thoughts for her, he thought angrily. No wonderings. No out-of-the-ordinary experience.

Miles suddenly remembered his vow not to be a fool like Spencer. Not to fall in love with her or try to change her. To take what she had to offer and expect nothing more.

For a few ghastly moments, he thought he might have done just that. Fallen in love with her. But then common sense returned, and with it some straight thinking.

Stop deluding yourself, Miles. That wasn't love. That was still just lust, dressed up by Maddie to

*look and feel like something else. She's a witch,
isn't she? A caster of spells, a player of games.*

He smiled a coldly cynical smile as he climbed
from the bed and made his way into the en suite.

She would never fool him again with her multiple personalities, one minute a vamp, the next a
frightened virgin, then finally the loving bride on
her wedding night.

Miles had the full picture now. Maddie liked
being in control when it came to matters of sex and
men, could not bear a man to ever have anything
over her. He'd startled her tonight by calling her
bluff and subduing her through his physical
strength. And whilst she'd enjoyed it physically, in-
tellectually she hadn't liked it one bit!

So she'd immediately fought back the only way
she had left. By using her softly feminine side,
weaving an emotion-charged spell to make him
succumb to *her* wishes rather than the other way
around. She'd cleverly tapped into a universal
weakness. Most men—most human beings, damn
it—wanted to be loved. The wicked witch had
tempted him with sex cleverly disguised as love, and
he'd allowed himself to become momentarily
bewitched.

The spell was broken now, thank God. In future,
he would recognise those particular tactics and not
be drawn in by them. Or alternatively, he might
even turn the tables and use the same tactics against
her. She was a human being, too, wasn't she? And
a woman, to boot. What women didn't want to
be loved?

Ah, yes. He'd learned a valuable lesson tonight from an expert. When all else failed, turn on the tenderness. After all, he'd not come all this way just for one night. He wanted Maddie in his bed every single weekend for the next six months!

Miles flushed the white toilet and stepped into the white shower, snapping on the water. He began to hum as he lathered up his body. Yes, he had Maddie all worked out now.

People always said knowledge was power.

They were right.

Maddie woke to the sound of the shower running. For a split second she was disoriented, but then the events of the evening came flooding back and her hands rushed to cover her face.

'Oh, God,' she groaned. 'God . . .'

She didn't know whether to laugh or to cry, to be appalled by what had happened or simply enthralled.

Miles, she thought, and let out a quavering sigh, her hands slipping away from her face.

He'd simply swept her off her feet and into another world, where she'd been a willing slave to his male demands, a puppet pushed this way and that for his oh so greedy mouth, first on her neck and then . . . oh, God, she could hardly bear to think of it.

She'd never allowed any man to do that before for so long. Briefly, yes, while she gritted her teeth and pretended to enjoy it.

But there'd been no pretence here on this bed. She'd revelled in every horribly intimate moment, intoxicated by the sensations his busy tongue and knowing fingers could create, stunned by the spasms of pleasure that had shaken her very core over and over and over.

So now you know what an orgasm's like, Maddie girl, came a caustic little voice.

She'd heard about them. Read about them. But now she knew.

It explained so much.

In the past, when she'd been forced to listen to other women waxing lyrical about the delights of sex, she'd been highly sceptical of their boasts of unbelievable ecstasy and multiple orgasms. Flights of fantasy, she used to think cynically.

Now she could well understand why it was they threw themselves at certain men's feet. It was because those men could do what most men obviously could not—send women to heaven.

Clearly, Miles was one of those men.

It wasn't love, of course, as so many silly women—her own mother included—liked to believe. It was just chemistry, or sex, or whatever one liked to call it.

In that case, why did you give him that cow-faced smile? that same sarcastic little voice demanded. *Why did you start fantasising that he must really care about you to stop and protect you, or that in the end, he was making beautiful love to you and not just having sex?*

*Because underneath your so-called liberated views
you're still a female fool, that's why!* came the
crushing answer. *Grow up. You don't love Miles
and he doesn't love you. This is lust here. Pure,
unadulterated lust, the same thing that's been
making fools of people since God created Adam
and Eve.*

'Talking to yourself, Maddie?'

Maddie only just managed to stop herself
gasping, swiftly schooling her face into a bland expression as she rolled to face the bathroom.

He was standing, starkers, in the open doorway,
casually towelling himself down. His hair was
dripping wet, and droplets of water clung to the
fine matting of dark hair that covered all of his
chest and most of his body.

He looked good naked, and very male, with a
long, lean nicely proportioned body. His shoulders
were broad, his stomach flat and his hips slender.
His sperm-donor equipment was in fine shape, too,
Maddie noted ruefully, and he wasn't even aroused.

Maddie tried reducing Miles in her mind to just
that. A well-equipped sperm donor. But it was not
easy. When she looked at him she was overcome
with longing to be in his arms again. There was no
thought of plans, or babies, or the future. Just the
here and now of more lovemaking.

And what's wrong with that? came the defensive
argument. *Why shouldn't you indulge yourself
while you've got the chance? Who knows? You
might never find another man who can do for you*

what Miles does. Don't forget, he's going back to England in six months.

Something moved inside Maddie at these last two thoughts. It was a tightening, akin to pain or panic.

Immediately, old and very cynical tapes clicked on to combat this new and unacceptable weakness. *Of course there will be other men. Your mother found a myriad to satisfy her over the years! You don't need Miles especially, except for the job you first delegated to him. Just think of the great sex as an additional bonus. Stop questioning it. Stop trying to make it into anything more than it is.*

Enjoy him every chance you get, Maddie, came her final advice, *but never ever let him get the better of you, or imagine for one moment you might love him. You can see what kind of man he is. More of a man than the ones you've had before. Give Miles an inch and he'll take a mile! So no more marsh- mallow looks or mushy murmurings. Keep it sharp and keep it sassy.*

Gathering herself, Maddie lifted a single saucy eyebrow then let her eyes travel ever so slowly over every one of Miles's marvellous physical attributes. She was startled, then fascinated to see that her simply looking at him had an immediate effect.

'Just counting my blessings, lover,' she drawled. 'I think all my Christmases have come at once.'

'In February?' he returned dryly as he rubbed his hair with the towel, not bothering to hide his ever increasing arousal from her.

Maddie licked her lips before she could stop herself.

'Coming back to bed?' she asked huskily, her heart beginning to hammer in her chest.

'What about a cup of coffee first?' came his un-expected reply. 'Or better still . . . that other bottle of wine.'

'Wine?' she repeated as though she'd never heard of the word.

Miles smiled with dark triumph. If the witch thought he'd jump on her bones every time she said jump, then she had another think coming.

Actually, he no more wanted damned wine than he wanted a ten-mile jog at that moment. But he had to keep the upper hand in this, or he'd find himself in real trouble. God damn it, the moment she set those smouldering black eyes on him his flesh had danced to immediate attention. It was downright mortifying in the extreme.

'Wine it is, then.' Her returning smile was saucy as she swung her long legs over the side of the bed and stood up, her long, jet-black curls falling just short of her breasts. He wished her hair was longer, then he wouldn't have to be confronted with those perky breasts and their suck-me nipples.

Not that it would have mattered. For she tossed all her hair over her shoulders then strode boldly from the room, making no attempt to pick up any kind of robe or wrap on the way.

He watched her, envying her naturalness in her nudity. It had almost killed him to stand before her, desperately trying to ignore his arousal. Which was crazy, really. She obviously didn't mind. Hell, she was probably used to men walking around her house with a permanent erection.

Miles took only a few seconds to surrender to the dark thought that flashed into his head. Arming himself a second time, he went in search of his torment.

He found her standing naked at the kitchen counter, her long, slender fingers occupied opening the wine bottle, her lovely little white bottom wiggling as she strained to pull the cork out.

She gasped when he came up behind her and put his arms around her, then moaned softly when he started playing with her breasts.

'Miles, stop it,' she whispered shakily at last, though he knew she didn't mean it. Her nipples were like steel pokers against the palms of his hands.

He did as she asked—in a fashion—abandoning her breasts and moving down over her flat stomach. Her skin was incredibly soft, yet firm. He loved the feel of her muscles clenching tight as his hands slid over her taut buttocks, then lower to the backs of her firm white thighs.

'Miles!' she rasped as he moved inexorably closer to his ultimate target.

'Mmm?'

She gasped, then shuddered. 'Oh, God...'

His excitement soared at her tortured words, not to mention her hot, eager little body, which was already beginning to squirm under his touch.

'You've stopped opening the bottle,' he said in a surprisingly cool voice.

'I . . . I can't,' she returned weakly. 'Not while you're doing that.'

'Try.'

He thrilled to her ineffectual fumblings, plus her instinctive action to obey him. The sense of power that came over him was intoxicating, for she was like putty in his arms.

Her hands finally fell way from the wine bottle to hang limply at her sides. She sank into him, her breathing heavy.

'Miles, no,' she protested shakily when he eased her legs apart.

'It's all right.' He ground the words out in her ear, glad now that he'd thought of protection before leaving the bedroom. If he hadn't, he might not have been able to stop at this point. And God, he just had to have her. Right here and now!

He felt her tense, then abruptly surrender to his will, shuddering violently. The moment held a dark triumph, which he thought could never be bettered. He took her hands and spread them wide on the counter as he pushed into her, bending her forward slightly to penetrate deeper, exulting in her attitude of primitive submission.

This was how men took their women in less civilised cultures.

Miles could see its attraction. The man had total control, total power. There was no eye contact, no need for anything but the act itself. It was a purely physical union with nothing sought but pleasure.

It was all he wanted from her, he decided with gritted teeth as he pumped more vigorously. Nothing more. Ever.

But then, without a word of warning, everything changed.

She began to move with him, her arms somehow escaping his and reaching behind her head to cradle his with oddly loving hands. 'Oh, my darling,' she murmured throatily as she undulated with sensual urgency against him. 'My darling...'

Miles had often fantasised about her calling him darling in a moment of mad passion. But never, in all his dreams, had it sounded like that.

Once again, his immediate response was a gut-wrenchingly emotional one, although some very real physical responses followed. First, he began to groan, raw, naked sounds such as had never escaped his lips before.

They embarrassed him. But dear God, the way she was moving!

In desperation, he wrapped his arms around her and held her tightly, burying his face in her neck in a vain attempt to stop her moving as well as to muffle his humiliating groans.

But it was hopeless, for he was helpless—helpless against the power of her expertise. Somehow she continued to move deep inside herself, and in no time, he was crying out even more loudly with the ecstasy of it all.

For several tortuous seconds he minded—Miles had always been a quiet and controlled lover—but then Maddie's own guileless gasps of delight made him see the folly of his ways.

What the hell? he thought. Where was it written that a man has to make love in staunch silence? And where is it also written that it is unmanly to let the woman take the assertive role occasionally?

Obviously not in Maddie's book. And it wasn't going to be in his, in future. He was going to let her do anything she damned well wanted to do to him, and vice versa.

Go with the flow, Miles, he told himself. *You deserve it. You've put up with thirty-three years of hypocritic garbage at home, lived your life to everyone else's rules but your own, and it's time you stopped. Be true to yourself, Miles. Say what you want with this woman. Be what you want. That's what you've come all this way for, isn't it?*

He nuzzled her throat, kissing her flesh and revelling in the glowing embers of their tempestuous union.

'That was fantastic, wench,' he murmured. 'Simply fantastic.'

'We aim to please, oh lord and master,' she whispered in a husky voice. 'Is there anything else your heart desires this night?'

'I feel I am in need of a brief respite. I shall retire to the white bedchamber anon, to which you will shortly bring the wine and cheese. And don't bother to dress, wench. I haven't finished with you yet.'

'Your wish is my command, my lord.'

He laughed and kissed her on the ear. Oh, yes, this was the life! What a fool he'd been to live it any other way!

CHAPTER NINE

'ARE you sure you don't mind pushing the pram?' Carolyn asked. 'You're not getting tired? We've been trundling through this shopping mall for ages.'

It was Friday afternoon, and Maddie had taken the rest of the day off to help Carolyn shop for a dress for the christening on the coming Sunday. She'd found a lovely blue one, but no shoes to match, as yet. It was just after three.

'Are you kidding?' Maddie said, smiling at her friend. 'I haven't had this much fun in years. I think, however, it's time for a cup of coffee. Let's go in here.'

She directed the pram through the doorway of a nearby coffee lounge and headed for a roomy table. Baby Pamela slept sweetly on, confirming Maddie's new opinion that babies were not the little monsters she'd always thought.

Maddie simply adored her godchild-to-be, and the intelligent little darling seemed to reciprocate the feelings, being as good as gold every time Maddie nursed her or pushed her around in her pram. Carolyn said it was because she was hypnotised by Maddie's earrings, but Maddie did not go along with that. The dear child simply had great taste!

'Are you still bringing Miles to the christening on Sunday?' Carolyn asked after the waitress had departed with their orders for cappuccinos.

'Uh-huh. Why? Did you think I'd change my mind?'

'Well, it's been nearly a month now since your affair with him started. This will be the fifth weekend in a row that you've lived in each other's pockets. I was thinking he must surely have blotted his copybook by now. After all, Miles is even more of a silver-tail snob than Spencer was.'

'Well, no, he's not, actually,' Maddie said. 'Not at all.'

Carolyn was taken aback by Maddie's thoughtfully dreamy expression, then thrilled by it. 'Maddie Powers!' she exclaimed. 'You've finally fallen in love. Oh, I'm so happy for you!'

Maddie blinked before her dark eyes flashed exasperation at Carolyn. 'Don't be silly. Of course I haven't. You don't fall in love with men like Miles. In lust, maybe. He's a fantastic lover. I can't seem to get enough of him.'

Which was true. Each week, by Friday evening, she would be on tenterhooks waiting for him to arrive. When he did, she would practically strip him at the door, so great was her need by that time.

Frankly, she still found her behaviour with Miles hard to believe. All those years of pretending with men, of promising and not really delivering, of playing the seduction game, just for the power kicks she got out of it.

Well, there was no pretending now, no promises without delivering good and proper. As for the seduction game... seduction no longer came into it. She was more than willing to give Miles whatever he wanted, whenever he wanted it. He was not averse to her taking the assertive role, as well... when it took her fancy.

And it seemed to be taking her fancy more and more. Only last weekend she had tied Miles to the bed while he'd been dozing, then had her wicked way with him for hours afterwards. Miles had loved every moment of it, once he got used to the idea, even though his four silk ties would never be the same again.

'What are you going to do when he moves into his own place at Stanwell Park?' Carolyn asked. 'I know Vaughan's finished the building.'

'He certainly has. And Miles is tickled pink with it. Another fortnight and my job should be finished, as well. I have everything under control. What will I do when Miles moves in?' she repeated, shrugging nonchalantly. 'I might move in with him, though only temporarily and only at the weekends. Otherwise we'll spend all our time driving back and forth.'

'Maddie...'

'What?'

'You're, er, not still thinking of using Miles for... you know, what you told me that day at the hospital? I don't want to say it out loud,' she whispered. 'Someone might overhear.'

Maddie laughed. 'Heaven forbid!'

'Well?' Carolyn prompted when Maddie didn't go on. '*Are* you?'

Maddie looked oddly disconcerted, which wasn't like her at all. 'I was, but I just don't know any more. I didn't expect to like him as much as I do. I mean, he's not at all like I first imagined....'

'Funny you should say that. Vaughan says exactly the same thing. He's grown to genuinely like the man, which isn't like Vaughan. He rarely changes his opinion about a person midstream.'

'Miles is certainly an enigma,' Maddie mused. 'One minute he can look and act like a typical British blue blood, then the next he's carrying on like a good old Aussie male, surfing and swigging back beer over the barbie with the best of them. He's gone as brown as a berry, as well. You'd never guess he was English by looking at him. Of course, once he opens his mouth he gives the game away. Not that I don't love the way he speaks. He can say darling like no man I've ever known. It sends shivers right down my spine.'

Carolyn rolled her eyes. 'So he calls you darling now, does he?'

'Surely does. Not to mention wench, witch, hussy and harlot, as well as a thousand other less complimentary names.'

'But that's terrible!'

Maddie laughed. 'They're actually terms of endearment.'

'Don't sound like terms of endearment to me!'

'Well, maybe they're not. But they're only fun names. He doesn't really mean them.'

'I hope not,' Carolyn pronounced, her voice indignant. 'If I ever hear him calling you disrespectful names in my presence I'll give him a piece of my mind.'

Maddie smiled with affection at Carolyn, who, though a sweetie, was not in any way wishy-washy. She'd given Vaughan plenty of lip when she'd imagined—quite erroneously as it turned out—that he'd once been her own mother's lover. People often underestimated Carolyn. Perhaps it was her soft blonde hair and big blue eyes.

'You would, too, wouldn't you?' Maddie said wryly.

The cappuccinos arrived at that point, deflecting their conversation away from Miles. Maddie was rather relieved. She didn't want to analyse her feelings for Miles any more. She'd done enough of that herself. The time she spent with him was magical and fun. Being in love with him would definitely spoil all that, because she would start thinking in terms of his leaving her in the end. Maddie wasn't into heartbreak, certainly not over a man.

Neither did she want to churn over her earlier plans to have a baby by him. She would definitely put that on the back burner for a while. After all, what was the hurry? Miles wasn't going anywhere for a good while.

Both women sipped their coffee in a thoughtful silence, Carolyn the first to put her cup down.

'By the way, Maddie,' she began. 'What, er, are *you* going to wear to the christening? Are you going to buy something new?'

Maddie smiled. Carolyn was far too nice to come right out and ask her baby's godmother to wear something half decent. Or point out that Maddie's wardrobe didn't appear to contain such a garment.

Maddie leaned over and gave her friend's arm a reassuring pat. 'Now don't you go worrying. I promise not to disgrace or embarrass you next Sunday.'

'You would never do that, Maddie, no matter what you wore. I was just thinking of you and what Miles might say if you came dressed in one of your more, er, flamboyant outfits.'

'If Miles knows what's good for him,' Maddie said dryly, 'then he wouldn't say a damned thing. Not that I intend coming in a flamboyant outfit. I happen to own a lovely white suit, which a grateful dressmaking client gave me once as a thank-you gift, and which I've never found the right occasion for. This seems to be it.'

'That sounds lovely,' Carolyn agreed, smiling her relief. She'd had visions of Maddie arriving at the Church in a black leather mini, see-through blouse, thigh-high black boots and earrings down to her hips. 'Has Miles ever commented on the clothes you wear?' she asked out of curiosity.

Maddie grinned. 'I don't seem to wear very much when I'm around him.'

Carolyn laughed. 'You're shocking, do you know that?'

'Yes.' She'd even been shocking herself lately.

'And Miles never complains? About the things you say or the way you act?'

'The only time Miles complains is when I'm too tired to do it again.'

'Maddie!'

'Just kidding. Not that you can talk, Carolyn. I know Vaughan from days of old. He's no slouch in the bedroom department. I'll bet he has you pregnant again before you can say Jack Robinson. Now let's change the subject from sex to our stomachs. I have this sudden hunger for lasagne, chips and salad. What do you say?'

'God, no,' Carolyn groaned. 'I'm having trouble as it is, losing the extra pounds I put on during my pregnancy. Why do you think I had to buy a new dress?'

'What rubbish! You look gorgeous and womanly. Pregnancy has done wonders for you. I'd give my eye teeth for your curves. I'm all bones.'

'There's bones and bones, Maddie. Yours are very elegantly put together.'

'How sweet of you to say so, but no, I know I'm thin. Still, Miles seems to like me that way, and that's all that counts.'

Carolyn refrained from making a comment over this last remark. Maddie didn't seem to realise the implication behind her words.

She could deny it all she liked, but Carolyn knew that Maddie was in love. She'd been fairly glowing for weeks, and the cynical brittleness that used to emerge in her comments about men had entirely disappeared. Vaughan had told her that it was Miles this and Miles that in the office all the time, ad nauseam.

'Are you sure I can't tempt you with some food?' Maddie asked once she'd signalled the waitress over.

Carolyn sighed. She really was hungry. 'Well, maybe a toasted sandwich...'

Miles snapped off the computer screen and rose from behind his desk. It was after five, and he'd had enough. He wanted to be on his way. He wanted his Maddie.

His Maddie, he thought ruefully as he cleared his desk. What a misnomer that was. Maddie would never belong to any man. She was her own woman in more ways than one. Wildly wilful and wonderfully wanton.

The last month had been the best month of his entire life. Monday to Friday at the office was spent in bittersweet anticipation of the coming weekend. Then the weekend itself...

Miles never knew what to expect once he got down there. But it was invariably exciting and incredibly satisfying.

Maddie had a wild sexual imagination. He could not believe what she'd done to him the previous weekend. His skin still prickled at the memory, though at the time, he'd wallowed in everything she did, then happily begged her for more.

He was totally besotted with her, no doubt about it. Whether he would still be in another five months was another matter. He would cross that bridge when he came to it. Maddie lived for the moment, and so would he.

His only worry was that she might grow bored with him before his time was up. He didn't want that. Hell, no. So he'd taken steps to avoid such an occurrence.

Opening the top drawer of his desk, he drew out a long black velvet case and slipped it into his jacket pocket, smiling as he thought of what lay within. He knew he'd chosen well. Women always liked diamonds, but this...this was special. As special as the woman it would adorn.

He wouldn't give it to her tonight, though. He didn't want to hold up her usual passionate greeting at the door. He'd give it to her sometime tomorrow, when the time was right.

Miles pictured her in his mind wearing nothing but his gift as she rode him. His flesh stirred, and he swore. *Not yet, you fool. You've at least a two-hour drive through heavy Friday night traffic before you arrive in Thirroul.*

Miles snatched up his car keys and headed for his private lift. Fifty minutes later, the city was behind him and he was on his way—to Maddie.

CHAPTER TEN

'MILES, will you sit still?' Maddie said impatiently. 'And stop staring at me. It's unnerving to try to paint a person when they keep staring at you.'

'And it's damned hard not to when someone's painting you in the nude,' Miles countered from where he was sitting, lotus-style, on the red velvet divan. 'Will you kindly go and put some clothes on?'

'Not on your nelly!' she refused, laughing. 'This was your idea, remember? You said if you had to take your clothes off, then so did I. Now be a good boy and close your eyes, or I'll paint them in, then everyone and his dog will know who my model was!'

'*Was* being the operative word,' Miles snarled, unfolding his legs and standing up. He'd sat in that stupid position for what felt like hours over the last four weekends, and he'd had enough. 'I renege. To hell with the Whitbread Prize. I'll *give* you whatever first prize is worth!'

Maddie put the paintbrush down with a sigh.

'Miles, darling,' she said reasonably enough. 'Why don't you come over here and take a peek at what I've done before throwing in the towel?'

Miles wasn't sure if he wanted to look at all. He simply didn't know what to expect. Finally, he told himself not to be such a coward and strode over.

'Good Lord!' he exclaimed, startled. 'That's not me!'

'It's *my* vision of you,' Maddie said defensively.

With a second long look, Miles could vaguely recognise himself in the nude figure on the canvas. The pose was certainly the same, the man in the portrait sitting cross-legged with his hands curled over his knees and his spine ramrod straight, his eyes discreetly shut as though he were meditating.

But there, any semblance stopped. The man in the painting had superbly defined, gleamingly bronzed muscles, giving rise to the image of some naked slave girl just off-canvas having recently oiled him all over.

It was, in fact, a powerful painting. Maddie had made him look almost mystical, yet given him an animal sexuality that Miles found both flattering and frustratingly infuriating. On that darned canvas, he looked the way he *wanted* to look yet never would.

'I'm not that brown,' he muttered. 'Nor that musclely.'

'You certainly are. Have you looked at yourself in the mirror lately?'

Was she kidding? Did she honestly think men ponced around naked in front of mirrors, admiring themselves?

'And what happened to my body hair?' he complained.

'I didn't paint any in. It spoilt the look I wanted. It's called poetic licence, Miles, only in this case, it applies to a painting.'

'Speaking of hair, you've also got me wearing a damned wig!' he said, sounding totally disgusted. He glared at the offending hair, which flowed down over the gleaming bronzed shoulders, the long dark waves thick and glossy and very sexy-looking. Miles *hated* every one of them. They set off bad tapes in his head.

'That's what you'd look like with long hair,' she was saying. 'It would suit you.'

'In your dreams, lover. I'm *never* going to grow my hair.'

'Why not?'

His laugh was not quite nice. 'Why not? Can you imagine what my business colleagues would say if I waltzed into the office looking like a refugee from an advertising agency? I'd be laughed out of the place.'

'Really? I thought you were the boss. I thought you could do as you pleased, and they would all still bow down and kiss your feet.'

'To my face, yes. But behind my back, they'd laugh themselves silly.'

'Who cares what they do behind your back? Who cares what they think?'

Miles stared at her, then shook his head. She really was incredibly naive, despite everything. The corporate world had rules, the same as society. Maddie might have found some hideaway niche down here where she could throw caution to the winds without consequence, but that sort of Bohemian behaviour would not wash in *his* world.

'You don't know what you're talking about,' he snapped.

Her eyes flashed and her chin shot up. 'Oh, yes, I do. I know exactly what I'm talking about. I've been around men like you all my life! I've seen them come and go. I've watched them stress themselves silly over the stupidest things then have coronaries or develop ulcers. And for what? For whom?'

'For money, you fool!' he countered savagely. 'And for their families! Where in hell do you think most men would get in this world if they didn't toe the conservative line? Not everyone can cocoon themselves down here in Shangri-la, Maddie, doing and saying whatever they please. Not forever. In the end, you have to go back to the real world, like I do every Monday morning. You're damned fortunate to have Vaughan as your partner and a friend. Believe me when I say not too many business colleagues would tolerate your mode of dress or general behaviour.'

'Is that so?' She crossed her arms and settled the coldest look upon him.

'Yes, that's so. And you know it!'

'How can I know anything, being a damned fool?'

'What in hell are you talking about?'

'That's what you just called me. And you're probably right. I must be a fool to have anything to do with a pain in the butt like you!'

Miles squeezed his eyes shut. My God, what was he doing? Worse, *why* was he doing it? He didn't want to fight with Maddie, or alienate her, or upset her. Hell, if he didn't have these weekends with her he would go mad. More and more he hated his corporate existence. More and more...

'I'm sorry,' he apologised gruffly. 'I didn't mean it. I was angry.'

When he went to take her into his arms, she resisted for a moment before suddenly hugging him to her chest. 'And I'm sorry, too. I didn't mean to make you angry. I *am* a fool.'

'No, I'm the fool, Maddie,' he said soothingly, stroking her hair and her back. 'Because I know in my heart you're right. I have to get out. I have to do something else for the rest of my life. But what?'

He felt Maddie stiffen in his arms and wondered what was behind it. Was she worried he might suddenly come the heavy with her? Declare his love and ask her to marry him?

Vaughan had laughingly told him one day that every time Maddie's current lover fell in love with her, she dumped him. It had been a friendly warning, but one he'd taken to heart, because he suspected it to be true. Maddie didn't want love and commitment from a man. Maddie only wanted fun and sex.

The trouble was, Miles suspected he *was* falling in love with her. He was also falling in love with her way of life, plus the way she *looked* at life. He adored being with her, and not just in bed. He loved talking to her and walking with her. He loved her mind as well as her body. He loved her delicious sense of humour and her wacky ways. Hell, he just loved her.

The acceptance of his true feelings brought with it a calmness he hadn't felt in ages, plus a fierce determination. He would win her heart as well as her body. He would leave no stone unturned in his pursuit of her. Then, when he revealed his love, she would not dump him. She would marry him, God damn it. He would not accept no for an answer. Maddie was going to be Mrs. Miles MacMillan.

'Maddie,' he murmured, his arms tender as he cuddled her to him.

'Yes?'

'Nothing. I just want to hold you.'

'Really?' She sounded surprised and a touch sceptical.

'Yes. And I really *do* like the painting. I think it's great, and I think you're a fantastic artist.'

'Yes, I know.'

He pulled back and scowled at her. 'You're an egotistical little devil, do you know that?'

'Takes one to know one. Now, are you going to resume the pose and let me get on with this masterpiece?'

'Do you think you could continue without me for a short while? The waves are looking extra good this afternoon.'

Maddie rolled her eyes at him. 'Truly, Miles, this obsession of yours with conquering the Australia surf is getting a bit much. Next thing I know, you'll be buying a surfboard.'

'Could be, Maddie, love,' he said as he stepped into his trunks and pulled them into place. 'But not till after I've mastered my bodysurfing technique.'

Her sigh was teasing and not serious. 'Off you go, then, and play your macho games. Far be it from me to try to change the male species and their compulsion for dangerous pastimes. But if you get severely dumped then don't come crying to me. The waves have a tendency to turn nasty at this time of day, so be warned!'

'Yes, Mummy,' he said mockingly. 'I promise to be careful.'

She pulled a face at him. 'The day I start mothering a man will be the day I see a psychiatrist!'

Miles laughed, took her shoulders and gave her a peck on the forehead. 'I'll remember you said that. See you soon.'

He ran out across the narrow backyard and onto the beach beyond, his long legs carrying him quickly across the sand. Maddie had turned to her painting before he hit the water.

It was over twenty minutes before she looked up again, a frown gathering on her forehead when she glanced at the ocean and couldn't immediately see Miles either in the water or on the beach. A sick little feeling formed in her stomach as her gaze searched fruitlessly for him among the high and quite rough waves.

The stretch of beach opposite Maddie's house was not one where swimming was advised, as there was quite a strong rip, not to mention a shelf of

sand on which the waves sometimes curled over and
dumped down with considerable force. Sensible
people always swam farther down, nearer the surf
club, where two flags indicated the safest area for
swimming and lifesavers were at the ready to rescue
anyone who got into difficulty.

Miles, being a typical egotistical male, dismissed
such a possibility where he was concerned.

'I'm a very strong swimmer,' he had told her the
first time she warned him about surfing outside the
flags.

He was, too. And his surfing skills had improved
out of sight. But no one was invincible, and the sea
could be very cruel.

Gulping down her growing panic, Maddie
covered her nakedness with the red silk bathrobe
she'd been wearing earlier, sashed it tightly and
dashed into the backyard. She stopped at the edge
of the sand, knowing that its heat would burn the
delicate soles of her feet. Her eyes searched for a
sight of Miles's dark head bobbing between the
waves, but in vain. There were no heads at all in
the water, let alone Miles's.

The possibility that he might be drowning somewhere out there brought with it a distress so great,
Maddie cried out loud. She launched herself across
the sand, no longer caring about the heat, ob-
livious of any pain except the pain in her heart.

'No,' she sobbed as she flew towards the water,
anxious eyes darting everywhere.

The water was cold, but she didn't care. She
charged right in, calling out his name as she waded

through the surf till she was waist deep. Her heart was thudding madly behind her ribs, her anguish forming a vice-like constriction within her chest.

Dear God, she must love the man to feel like this. This couldn't be just lust. It had to be love!

The brush of some seaweed against her legs almost gave her a heart attack. She'd thought it was a body in the water for a moment.

Tears were streaming down her face.

'Oh, Miles!' She choked the words out. 'Where are you, you fool?'

'Right here behind you.'

She whirled, her mouth falling open at the sight of his standing there in the shallows, his upper body not even wet. He was also staring at *her* as though she were mad.

Which she was. Quite mad. She had to be, to fall in love at all, let alone with Miles!

Her relief at finding him alive was quickly overwhelmed by frustration at her own stupidity.

'And where the hell have *you* been?' she demanded, stomping out of the water with furious strides. 'I thought you'd gone and broken your silly damned neck or something.'

'Nope. The surf was a bit rough, so I got out and went for a jog to dry off. I'd forgotten to bring a towel, you see.'

Maddie ground to a waterlogged halt in front of him and clamped her hands on her hips. 'He'd forgotten his towel!' she mimicked savagely. 'Do you realise you've been gone nearly half an hour? Didn't you think I might be worried when you didn't come back in ten minutes?'

Miles smiled. 'Watch it. You're beginning to sound like a mother again.'

'Mother, my foot. I'm merely protecting my investment!'

A sardonic eyebrow lifted. 'Your investment?'

'Of course. Where am I going to get another subject for the Whitbread Prize at this late stage? Besides,' she added tartly, 'I've grown accustomed to your face. Not to mention certain other parts of your anatomy.'

Miles laughed. 'That's a relief. I thought you were referring to your contract to decorate my house.'

'Don't be ridiculous! I don't need to decorate a man's house to secure him as my lover.'

'I can believe that,' he said dryly, his eyes raking over her.

It was only then that Maddie realised the sodden robe was gaping dangerously apart. Why she blushed, she had no idea. There wasn't anyone else around to see. Their stretch of beach was deserted.

Miles suddenly surged through the water and grabbed her. His mouth was hot on hers, his hands sliding up underneath the robe to cup her cold, wet buttocks and press her around his rapidly burgeoning arousal.

Maddie froze under his aggressive lovemaking, fighting the urge to blindly surrender, afraid of where her relationship with Miles would lead her, now that she loved him.

Miles totally misinterpreted her momentary resistance and swept her into his arms. 'I understand,' he rasped as he carried her out of the water and towards the house. 'You like privacy for your sex. And protection.'

Protection...

That almost made Maddie laugh. Was he going to protect her heart as well as her body?

She doubted it.

She doubted all sorts of things. But it was impossible to keep worrying about the future once they were alone inside and in each other's arms. Loving Miles gave making love with him a deeper meaning, a more intense arousal and an even sharper pleasure.

The present was far too exciting for negative thoughts, Maddie decided. She would think about where their relationship was going later on this evening. Or better still... in the morning.

CHAPTER ELEVEN

'MY, DON'T you look handsome!' Maddie compli-
mented airily as she breezed into the kitchen Sunday
morning. He was, too. Heart-stoppingly so, in a
teal blue suit that made his grey eyes seem almost
blue.

She'd almost come to terms with loving Miles and
was not going to fight her feelings. Such struggling
was futile, anyway. Every time he touched her, she
simply melted. Truly, last night, she had not been
able to get enough of him.

In the end, Maddie had sensibly decided to enjoy
whatever time she had with him, and she hoped she
would have enough maturity not to crack up when
their affair ended in another five months.

Naturally, she was not going to let Miles know
the depths of her feelings. She was not that much
a fool. She'd seen for herself what happened when
a woman told a man like Miles she loved him. She
started being taken for granted, used and abused
in various ways. Maddie was not about to give any
man knowledgeable power over her, so it was
critical that she maintain a facade of lustful nonchalance whenever they were together.

'So why are you dressed so early?' she asked him
as she put the electric kettle on. 'The christening
isn't till eleven.'

'It's gone ten,' he pointed out.

'So? The church is only ten minutes away. I'm showered and made up. I'll put my clothes on at ten forty and we'll be off by ten forty-five.'

'That's cutting it a bit fine, don't you think?'

'Perhaps. Okay, I'll dress at ten forty-three.'

Miles rolled his eyes. 'Thank God she doesn't catch planes,' he muttered.

'You really should stop talking to yourself, darling,' she mocked as she poured herself her third cup of coffee since staggering out of bed around nine. 'It's the first sign of madness, you know.'

'Maybe I *am* mad.'

'Aren't we all,' she murmured.

It had been a torrid night, and quite crazy at times. Maddie had no idea she was so... athletic.

She hadn't felt too athletic when she first woke this morning, with every muscle in her body protesting loudly. It reminded her of the morning after she'd been horse riding on her twenty-first birthday... for the first and last time.

Maddie knew, however, that she would return to another type of riding. She'd become infinitely addicted to the sight of Miles lying beneath her, his handsome face consumed by a passion that seemed as driven as her own.

But only *seemed*.

Maddie's cynicism over men like Miles was considerable. Their obsession with women outside their social circle was only sexual, a fantasy-style passion that had a limited life span. Not for them any real love, even though they sometimes imagined they were in love. Maddie's mother had foolishly always believed her wealthy lovers when they declared their undying devotion. Invariably, they moved on once the lust began to wear off, leaving a devastated woman behind.

Maddie had learned to move them on herself before that happened, thereby satisfying some deep need inside herself to show men that they would never do that to her. Never!

But dear God, she'd never imagined for one moment she would fall in love with one of them, that she would ever need a man with a need that didn't listen to the voice of bitter experience. What would she do when Miles went back to England? How would she survive without him?

Maddie swept up her coffee mug with a burst of self-disgust, spilling a little onto the counter. She scowled at the spreading stain. See where being in love gets you?

Taking a deep, steadying breath, Maddie wiped up the stain, then steadfastly put her mind to living one day at a time and enjoying it for what it was. To start worrying about the future was futile.

'You know, I have no idea why Carolyn asked me to be Pamela's godmother,' she said quite brightly over the rim of the steaming mug. 'You can't get a more godless person than me. I *was* christened as a wee babe, but I haven't been in a church since the year dot.'

'Don't be ridiculous, Maddie,' Miles refuted firmly. 'Godliness has nothing to do with formal religion. It has to do with one's basic goodness.

And you're a very good person. I think you're a fine choice as godmother.'

Maddie eyed him cynically. 'You don't really mean that, Miles.'

'I certainly do. So who have they asked to be the godfather?'

'And old surfing mate of Vaughan's. His name is Wayne. They go back many years.'

'I thought he might have asked Julian.'

'I think he thought Julian was a bit old for the job. Besides, he's the babe's grandfather.'

'Fair enough. So what is the godmother going to wear today?'

Maddie stiffened, then slowly put down her coffee mug. She'd been waiting for this moment. Their first public appearance together. Miles's first real chance to criticise her clothes.

Good, she thought. *I won't love him quite so much once he starts picking on me.*

'Does it matter?' she asked, her tone challenging.

'I think it does . . . on this occasion.'

'Why?'

'You know why, Maddie. There is a time and place for everything. And a christening in a church—especially when one is the godmother—is not a place for black leather, skimpy skirts and bare legs.'

'Is that so?'

'Yes, that's so. Now stop trying to get a rise out of me and tell me what you're wearing. I'm sure it will be something very appropriate and elegant.

And I'm sure I'm going to be very proud of you today.'

Maddie couldn't help it. She melted, all her defiance draining away. If he'd been pompously pontifical, like Spencer, or scathingly sarcastic like other men she'd known, then she would have torn strips off him. Instead, he'd been awfully clever, she thought, hiding sneaky compliments within his sensible remarks.

Beneath her involuntary pleasure, she suspected he was buttering her up only to get his own way later, but she still couldn't help responding.

'Well, I do have this white suit,' she heard herself saying in the sort of sweet tones she hadn't used in a decade. But damn it all, she did so desperately want to please him. And she wanted him to be proud of her in public. There! She admitted it! She didn't want him thinking she looked cheap. She wanted him to be as proud of her as he would be of one of his English roses back home.

'That sounds perfect, Maddie,' he returned with a dazzling smile. 'I can't wait to see it on you.'

She raced off to put on the white suit, then hurried back to bask in his approval. It was a very classically tailored outfit, with a straight skirt that finished just above the knees and a fitted jacket with short sleeves, a sweetheart neckline and covered buttons down the front. Maddie had put her hair up, though dozens of wispy curls dangled around her face and down her neck. She wasn't wearing earrings for once, as she didn't have anything that matched.

'Oh, Maddie,' Miles said warmly, his eyes gleaming with real admiration. 'You look lovely. I think white suits you even more than black does. I'm going to take you out next week and buy you a dozen white outfits.'

'Oh, no, you won't,' she told him straight. As much as she wanted to please Miles, there were some rules she refused to bend. 'It's not Christmas or my birthday. I never accept presents from men except on those occasions.'

Miles frowned. 'Never?'

'Well, I don't count things like flowers or boxes of chocolates. I was talking about expensive presents. The kind that might make one think one is being paid for services rendered.'

'Oh, *that* kind. Well, the small gift I bought for you this week shouldn't make you think that. It wasn't *that* expensive.'

'You . . . you've bought me a gift?' Maddie could not help being touched. 'What is it?'

'Just a pair of earrings. Though I'm not sure they would go with that outfit. When I bought them I was picturing you wearing them with, er, something different. Wait here. I'll get them. Do we have time?'

'A few minutes.'

Miles dashed off to the bedroom, thanking his lucky stars that he hadn't given them to her before, or he'd have really put his foot in it. He snatched the diamond-drop earrings out of the giveaway expensive box and returned to the kitchen, holding them up as though they were a two-dollar purchase from some flea market.

Maddie gasped when she saw them. 'Oh, Miles, they're gorgeous. Wherever did you get them? They look real.'

'That's what I thought. They're zircons,' he lied bravely.

Maddie frowned. 'I can believe that. They say you sometimes can't tell the difference with zircons. But I've heard they can be a bit expensive, too. I hope you didn't pay too much for them.'

'Only a couple of hundred.'

Her mouth gaped open. 'Only a couple of hundred! But that's outrageous. You were ripped off.'

'Oh, I don't think so. The workmanship is very good. And I can afford it.'

'That's not the point. I'll bet you waltzed into one of those city jewellery shops dressed in one of your fancy suits and the man behind the counter immediately thought to himself, Here comes a ripe one! If I didn't love these earrings to death I'd make you take them right back and get a refund.'

Miles's heart turned over. God, but he loved this woman. She made Annabel look like a greedy, grasping cow.

'You like them then?' he asked.

'I adore them! I'm going to wear them whether they go or not.' And she slipped them onto her ears.

'And *I* adore *you*,' he rasped, pulling her into his arms.

Their eyes met, and Miles was sure he saw a startled delight in hers before a dryly amused cynicism crept back in.

'I know what *you* adore, Miles MacMillan.'

He laughed. 'That, too. But it's more than just sex, Maddie. Don't you like me for more than just the sex?'

'What are you up to?' she demanded.

Damn, but she was a suspicious creature. Not for the first time, he wondered what was behind her unwillingness to commit herself to a man except briefly and then only physically. If he had the opportunity today, he might ask Vaughan—or maybe Carolyn—to fill him in with a few details of Maddie's background.

He sure as hell wasn't going to pry them out of Maddie. When it came to talking about herself or her upbringing, she was a closed shop. He'd tried once when they were lying together in bed after making love, but she quickly changed the subject, then distracted him totally with that incredibly sexy body of hers.

Speaking of which...

He went to kiss her, but she wrenched out of his arms, looking just a little flustered, he thought, which was odd for Maddie.

'We haven't time for this,' she said sharply. 'We have to be going.'

He watched her spin agitatedly away and wondered what had upset her. But then he shrugged and simply followed. No point in trying to work Maddie out. She was too complex for guesses. He needed information. And he aimed to get it. Today.

CHAPTER TWELVE

'I DON'T know what it is about you, Maddie,' Vaughan said after the christening was over. 'But you only have to come within three feet of Pamela, and she turns into an absolute angel. Even with me she cries occasionally, but with you...she either smiles, stares silently or sleeps. What's your secret?'

'It's the earrings, Vaughan,' Carolyn insisted. 'She hypnotises Pammie with them. Speaking of which, I couldn't help but admire the gorgeous ones you've got on today, Maddie. Wherever did you get them? If I didn't know better, I'd say they were real diamonds!'

'Miles gave them to me,' she told them, glancing over to where he was happily chatting to Julian and Isabel. 'But they're not diamonds, they're zircons.'

'Are you sure?' Carolyn asked, frowning. 'I mean, Mum's got some diamond earrings, and I could have sworn yours were just as real.'

'Now, why would Miles give me real diamonds and tell me they were zircons, Carolyn?' Maddie said. 'That doesn't make any sense. Does it, darling?' she crooned at her godchild, who was lying contentedly in her arms, not making a peep. 'Are we going back to your place for the goodies, Carolyn, or your mother's?'

'Mum's. Our place hasn't recovered yet from parenthood, has it Vaughan? Besides, Mum's is larger.'

'I hope you're not talking about my bottom,' Isabel said with mock horror as she joined them.

'No. Your house,' Maddie told her.

'That's a relief! I was looking at my expanding derriere in the mirror this morning and thinking I'd have to either take up jogging or go on a diet. Or both!'

'What rubbish, Isabel,' Maddie said. 'You have a lovely figure. I wish I had a bit more meat on *my* bottom. And on other parts of my anatomy.'

Carolyn groaned. 'Let's not start talking about bottoms and boobs. I think mine are going to be the death of me. And I used to be such a skinny little thing before I had a baby.'

'You were no such thing!' Vaughan refuted. 'And I have proof, hanging over my bed. You were always lovely and shapely, my sweet,' he said, hugging her to his side. 'Now, no more talk of diets. Here, Maddie, give me the baby. She must be getting heavy by now. Let's off to the party, everyone. Wayne! Lisa!' he called to the godfather and his girlfriend. 'We're off to Julian's place. Now where is Julian? And Miles, too, for that matter?'

'Standing right behind you, Vaughan,' Maddie said as her eyes met Miles's narrow-eyed look over Vaughan's shoulder. He seemed to be watching her all the time today. Watching and waiting. But for what?

As for her part, being with Carolyn's baby again had brought back those untapped maternal feelings with a rush. The urge to have a baby was stronger than ever. The compulsion to have Miles's baby was even stronger.

Maybe she wouldn't die of heartbreak after he went back to England if he left a small part of himself behind....

'So now I know the secret of the nude above Vaughan's bed!' was the first thing Miles said when they were alone in her car. 'Your model was Carolyn.'

'Yes, of course. Who did you think it was? Oh, Lord!' She laughed. 'You thought if was Vaughan!'

'For pity's sake watch the road, will you?' Miles gasped as the car drifted dangerously close to the rock face on his immediate left. 'And slow down! God, I should have insisted on bringing my car. And yes, of course I thought it was Vaughan! Every time I took my clothes off these past few weeks to pose for you I kept imagining you painting him naked, and of being with him naked.'

'Ooh, I like you jealous,' she told him, smiling smugly. 'You're so deliciously impassioned. It's almost a pity that Vaughan and I have never been lovers. I could have milked it for all it's worth.'

'Well, if you've never been lovers, then what *are* you, damn it? Where did you meet? What have you shared? Do you realise I know nothing about you, Maddie, except what I've been able to glean along the way? You never tell me anything about your past.'

'I haven't noticed you giving me a minute-by-minute description of the last thirty-three years of *your* life, Miles,' she countered dryly. 'Which is exactly the way I like it. I don't need to know a man's life history to enjoy being with him, and vice versa. I don't want to understand you, Miles. I'm not your wife.'

'Neither are you likely to be,' he muttered frustratedly.

'Exactly.'

'That's not what I meant, damn you.'

'Why don't you quit while you're ahead, Miles? You're a fantastic lover, but I'm no more going to marry you than you're going to marry me. So please don't feel you have to go all deep and meaningful on me to keep our affair going. There's no need to play "I'll tell you my life story if you tell me yours." To begin with, mine's as dull as ditch water, and yours will only make me either envy or despise you. Look, if you want out, just say so,' she said coldly. 'I won't try to hold you against your will.'

Miles wished he hadn't started this conversation at all. He could feel her anger beneath the frosty facade.

'I don't want out,' he muttered unhappily.

'In that case stop trying to change the status quo,' she snapped. 'Believe me when I tell you trying to change me brings out the worst in me.'

'So I've been told.' And so he was seeing for himself!

'Vaughan been talking to you again?'

'No, Carolyn. I sat next to her in the church.'

'And you pumped her for information about me?'

'I wouldn't say that, exactly.'

'I would. So what did you learn?' She bit the words out. 'That I'm all bitter and twisted about men because my flowerchild hippie mother got herself knocked up then dumped by some married politician?'

Miles cringed inside when Maddie glowered at him. For that was exactly what Carolyn had told him, though a little more delicately.

'I can see by the look on your face that's pretty well what she said. Dear Carolyn doesn't know the half of it. I never told her about all the other politicians who shared my mother's bed during my growing-up years. She lives conveniently close to Canberra, you see, but far enough out of town for her male visitors not to be spotted. A lot of *them* turned out to be married, as well, and *all* of them were filthy liars. They always told her they loved her. Some even promised marriage.

'But all they wanted from her was sex, the bastards!' she swept on, her voice full of contempt. 'After they'd had their fill, they would leave her crying and crushed, and I would have to pick up the pieces. God, I could never understand why she kept believing their lies time after time. How many times, I used to agonise, before she finally realised what she was dealing with?'

Miles was appalled, both by the picture Maddie was painting of her girlhood and the problem her well-justified cynicism over men presented to him.

He would have great difficulty winning her trust and her love. It was almost a mission impossible.

'And she's still damned well doing it!' Maddie raved on. 'Still letting herself be lied to and laid with regular monotony. It makes me so mad because she's such a beautiful person. A sweet, kind, generous soul who's constantly being taken advantage of simply because she wants to be loved.

'Love,' Maddie said scornfully with her top lip curling. 'I wouldn't give you two shillings for what most men call love!'

With her tirade over, an awkward silence descended in the car. Miles didn't know what to say. He felt totally depressed. No point in telling her he loved her now. It would be a waste of time.

But actions speak louder than words, he recalled his grandmother telling him once. A man is known for his deeds!

Miles decided then and there he would *show* the woman he loved her, not tell her.

But how? he wondered. Making love to her was not the way—though he wasn't about to slow down on that score. Not after last night. Last night had been out of this world. He'd never known such uninhibited passion!

Giving her gifts was not the way, either. She would think he was trying to corrupt her, or buy her. Which left ... what?'

Time, he decided, and tenderness.

'I've been thinking, Maddie,' he began as the car started chugging up the steep mountain road that led to Julian's house. 'I really need a decent break away from the company. I've been working eighteen-hour days six days a week for years. So I've decided to have a real holiday for the rest of my stay out here. There's plenty of talented fellows in Australia who can successfully run the Sydney branch. They don't need me. And another thing. When I move into my new house down here next weekend, Maddie, I want you to move in with me.'

Her head whipped round in surprise—not a wise move on this narrow, winding road. The car hit the strip of gravel on the side of the road, the wheels spinning, the back of the car swerving left and right. It was hairy for a few seconds before Maddie regained control of the vehicle.

Once they were safe, Miles expelled the air that shock had sent into his lungs. 'God, Maddie!'

'Serves you right for springing surprises on me on this road,' she said dryly. 'As for your proposition...I'm sorry, Miles, but I don't live with men.'

'I'm not asking you to live with men,' he said, holding his temper with great difficulty. 'I'm asking you to live with me.'

'Same thing.'

'No, it's not.' Miles realised he would have to be very cunning if he wanted Maddie to move in with him. 'I'm not asking for commitment or permanency. Neither am I asking you to look after me in any housekeeping sense. I'm simply asking for your companionship on a more convenient basis. My house is a fair way from yours, and we'd be driving back and forth all the time. Considering your driving skills and the state of this car, I think it would be best all round if we lived together for the duration of my stay in Australia.'

Her sidewards glance was irritatingly unreadable. 'So you won't expect me to pick up after you, or cook for you?'

'Never on the first question, and only if you want to on the second. I aim to learn how to cook myself. I'm going to make it one of my goals during the next five months.'

'And what are your other goals?'

He gave her as bland a look as she'd given him. 'To master riding a surfboard. And I'm going to try hang-gliding. I saw some chaps doing that off the cliffs at Stanwell Park last weekend when we inspected the house, and it looked like fun.'

Her glance showed alarm. 'Don't be silly, Miles. That's really dangerous. More so than surfing.'

'I'll be careful. I'll get proper lessons.'

'You'll break your silly neck before you're through,' she muttered.

'It's my neck to break,' he said, enjoying her obvious concern. Maybe she already cared about him more than she realised.

'You won't be much good to me in a hospital bed.'

Miles's disappointment in her reply brought a sharply dry rejoinder. 'I'm glad to see you've still got your priorities right where I'm concerned, Maddie. For a moment there, I thought you cared.'

'Silly Miles.'

Yes, silly Miles, he thought savagely.

'So are you going to move in with me or not?' he demanded, his tone having grown impatient with his thoughts.

'Well, yes, I think I just might.'

'She thinks she just might,' he repeated through gritted teeth. 'Don't put yourself out.'

'Oh, I won't. And speaking of putting myself out . . . What say—in the interests of convenience—I go on the pill? After we've exchanged medical clearances, of course.'

'Oh, of course!' came his caustic comment. 'I wouldn't want you taking any unnecessary risks.'

'Well, thank you, Miles, but I was thinking more of you. Men of your ilk can be real worriers about such matters.'

He could feel his blood pressure rising dangerously but battled to control it. Be damned if he was going to let her get to him. 'You really shouldn't generalise about men of my ilk, Maddie,' he drawled. 'We're not as easy to read as you think. And we don't come out of a mould.'

'Would I think that of you? Heavens, no. You're no cheap copy, Miles. You're unique. When God made you, he broke the mould. Why do you think I asked you to model for me?'

'I'm beginning to think it was simply to get me to take my clothes off.'

Her smile was rueful. 'Ah, he's found me out. And I thought I could keep on using the Whitbread Prize ruse forever and not be unmasked. Darling clever Miles, are you angry with me?'

Angry didn't begin to describe how he was feeling! 'Why should I be angry?' He tossed the question at her, congratulating himself on his nonchalance. 'I'm getting what I want, as well, aren't I?'

He glared through the passenger window to stop her from seeing the emotions on his face. Thankfully, she didn't keep the conversation going.

Still, Miles was relieved when they reached the crest of the hill and Julian's house came into sight. He wasn't sure if *he* could keep his mouth tactfully shut any longer. He wanted to rant and rave at her, to castigate her for letting her mother's experiences turn her into a cold-hearted cynic who looked to men for one thing only, simply because she didn't think them capable of any more depth.

That might be true of other men, but not him! He had plenty more to give her besides sex. Yet that was all she wanted.

Very well, he resolved stubbornly. That was what he'd give her.

But he'd also give her something else at the same time, whether she wanted it or not. He would give her his love. It would be there, in every kiss and caress, whispering to her subconscious, winning her over without her realising it.

Miles hadn't found someone as unique as Maddie simply to lose her over the unscrupulous actions of other men. She was going to be his, in every sense of the word. And if that meant *he* had to be a little unscrupulous, then so be it!

CHAPTER THIRTEEN

MADDIE wrapped her freshly showered and powdered body in a black silk robe, then pulled the towel from her head, letting her still damp curls tumble around her face and shoulders. Running her fingers through her hair, she left the bathroom and wandered into the bedroom, where she stopped for a moment and admired the painting on the wall opposite the bed.

What a shame Miles had not let her enter his painting in the Whitbread Prize! It would have won, for sure. Still, it was rather nice to hug his gorgeous body all to herself. She loved lying in bed and looking at it. Miles still grumbled it was nothing like him, but she noted he'd begun to let his hair grow, and each day the resemblance to the man in the painting increased.

Maddie blew him a kiss and went upstairs, smiling.

It looked breezy outside, and quite cool, while inside it was pleasantly warm. The sliding glass windows on both balconies were shut, and the slanting morning sunshine created a greenhouse effect, warming the whole house without having to use the airconditioning. You would never know winter was just around the corner.

Maddie made herself a mug of coffee and carried it into the main living area, where she curled up on one of the large leather armchairs that faced the view. She was content to just sit there, sip her drink and admire her own handiwork for the umpteenth time.

She'd done a fantastic job on Miles's house. There was no doubt about it. So good, in fact, that she infinitely preferred his place to her own. It was no hardship to live here with him in an aesthetic sense.

It was no hardship on *any* level.

Her eyes drifted to the floor. She hadn't chosen blue carpet, as he requested, for blue carpet was a notorious fader in the strong Australian light. Instead, she'd found some blue-veined Italian tiles and combined them with thick white scatter rugs, on top of which sat a peacock blue leather lounge and an assembly of glass-topped tables, which were as artistically decorative as they were practical. She'd also indulged her love of lamps, as opposed to harsher overhead lighting, choosing a wide variety with white bases and blending blue shades.

At night, the place glowed with a faintly blue sheen. Miles loved it, and so did she.

Maddie sighed at this last thought. The fact was, she loved the place too much. And Miles too much.

Who would have dreamt he'd be so easy to live with? And so considerate. And so damned *sweet*!

It was nearly three months since she'd moved in with him, and he was *still* doing nice little things for her. Bringing her cups of coffee in bed of a morning. Massaging her feet when she'd had a hard day. Buying her thoughtful little things, like posies of flowers and chocolates.

If one wasn't to know better, one would almost think he really loved her!

Maddie pulled a face at this last ridiculous thought, uncurled herself from the chair and was on her way to the kitchen with the empty mug when the telephone rang. There was no answering machine. Miles refused to have one. He wanted no reminder, he said, of office equipment.

Maddie hurried into the kitchen and snatched the extension on the kitchen wall. 'Yes,' came her brisk answer, empty mug still in hand.

'You're up.'

'Yes, Miles darling. At last.' She settled herself on a stool and put the mug on the white granite benchtop. 'Thank God for Saturday mornings, I say. And where are you? Has Julian taken you right off into the wilderness?'

'He certainly has. Don't ask me where I am. I have no idea. Somewhere south. Damned pretty place, though. I can see why Julian wants to buy land here. He's trying to talk me into going in with him.'

Maddie was startled. 'But... but you're going back home in two months. Are you sure you want to invest money into something so far away?'

'I might not go home in two months,' Miles said, totally taking her breath away.

Not go home? But he *had* to go home. She was already pregnant with his child. Or she suspected she was. She hadn't been to the doctor yet, not wanting to face what she had done for a while.

Now she had to face it.

'I was thinking of staying a little longer,' he added.

True panic set in. If Miles stayed in Australia too long, he might find out about her condition, and then there would be hell to pay! Maddie knew enough about Miles to know he'd be furious with her for tricking him. God, she felt guilty enough herself for telling him she was on the pill when she wasn't.

'Oh?' she said, panic making her sharp. 'This is the first I've heard of this.'

Miles suppressed a sigh. He'd hoped for a better reception to his news, hoped he'd made some headway with her over the past three months. No such luck. She was immediately on the defensive, one and one perhaps making two in her mind. He'd played his hand too quickly.

'It was just a thought,' he replied offhandedly. 'I probably won't. Actually, Max has been at me to come home earlier. He says I'm needed there.' *A damned sight more than I'm needed here, obviously!*

'Your brother's probably right,' Maddie said. 'Your mother won't be too happy if you don't go home when you planned, as well. She always sounds so lonely in her letters.'

Miles regretted reading them to her. It had been a vain attempt to get their relationship on a more intimate level. He'd never dreamt she would use the contents as emotional blackmail.

Was she getting bored with him? he wondered. Or had she sensed he'd fallen in love with her? Vaughan had warned him that that would be the kiss of death with her, but he'd been too bloody arrogant to believe him.

'Well, it's a nice change to be wanted,' he said testily.

'I always want you, Miles,' she said in a huskily seductive voice. 'You know that.'

Only for one thing, came his vicious thought.

No, darling Maddie wasn't bored, at least not with the sex part. Their love life had been even better since she'd gone on the pill. More spontaneous.

There wasn't a room in the new house where they hadn't made love. Or a time of day during which they hadn't indulged. Morning, noon or night. It made no difference.

Mostly, Maddie's insatiable appetite for him brought Miles great pleasure and satisfaction. Right at this moment, however, he bitterly resented both her desire for him and the way she could make him want her, even when he was furious with her.

'When are you coming home?' she asked. 'I'm missing you already.'

'God only knows. I'm at Julian's mercy, aren't I? I didn't bring my car. Late this afternoon, would be my guess.'

'Don't be too late,' she said, almost purring. 'I'm going to cook you something really special tonight.

We'll open a bottle of wine and have a lovely time. Now I must go, darling. I'm not long out of the shower and I'm beginning to get goose bumps. Bye, and don't go committing yourself to anything today. Think about it for a while first.'

Miles had a vision of her standing there in her birthday suit, her streamlined body all wet from the shower, her nipples all hard and glistening.

His groan was a mixture of frustration and irritation. He could not go on like this, he thought, agonised. He really couldn't. He felt like a puppet, pulled this way and that by her sexual strings.

Enough was enough, he decided. She would have him on *his* terms from this day forward, or not at all!

Maddie hung up, hating herself for having put on that vampish act with Miles. It had been a cheap, manipulative sham with not a shred of truth in it. She'd made him think she was naked, which she wasn't. She'd made him think she wanted him every minute of every day. Which she didn't.

Oh, yes, she wanted him. But it was the whole man she wanted, not just his body. She'd tried to control her feelings and their relationship by concentrating on the sex, but it hadn't worked. Not at all. She was more in love with him than ever. And now her outrageous behaviour had really backfired on her.

No doubt one of the reasons Miles was thinking of staying a little longer was to have more of the sex on tap she'd been giving him. There wasn't a man alive who would turn his back on the fantasy love life she'd been dishing up day after day after day.

But he was never going to give her what she'd begun to want. He was never going to stay here permanently and marry her.

What decent man would want to marry you? came the savage taunt. *You, with your cheap clothes and your cheap talk and your cheap ways?*

And Miles *was* decent. Much more so than she'd ever envisaged. He should *not* have been, with his background. He should have been more hopelessly arrogant and selfish and critical. Why in hell wasn't he?

Maddie was shocked when the tears started dripping off the end of her nose. She hadn't realised she was crying.

Weeping had not been a part of Maddie's daily routine for years. But once started, she couldn't seem to stop. Groaning, she dropped her head into her hands on the benchtop and cried her eyes out.

'Oh, Miles,' she sobbed aloud. 'Miles...'

The telephone ringing again jerked her out of her wretchedness. She glared at it for a moment as she dashed the tears away, then snatched it from the wall a second time.

Maddie tripped out a falsely bright hello.

'I would like to speak to Miles MacMillan,' said a voice with a Prince Charles accent. 'This is Max MacMillan. His brother.'

Maddie's eyebrows shot ceilingwards. This was a first. Miles's brother, actually calling him from England. He'd written once or twice, but never rung. She wondered what he wanted. Maddie had read between the lines of Miles's few comments about dear old Max, and she'd long decided she didn't like him any more than Miles did.

'Miles is not here, I'm afraid,' she said archly and uninformatively.

'And to whom am I speaking?'

Her eyes rolled at the pomposity of the man. 'My name is Madeline Powers,' she said in the most plummy accent she could rustle up. '*Ms* Madeline Powers.'

'So tell me, *Ms* Powers.' The voice almost sneered. 'What are you to my brother that you are answering his home telephone while he's not there? Cleaner? Housekeeper? Or mistress?'

Maddie dropped any attempt at culture. 'Decorator, actually,' she countered tartly. 'And friend. And live-in lover. What's it to you? You're not your brother's keeper, are you?'

When she heard him suck in a surprised breath, Maddie smiled. The gauntlets had been thrown down, and she was not about to back away. Maddie despised men like Max and would not pretend otherwise.

'I always have my brother's best interests at heart.' He pronounced the words stiffly. 'When will Miles be home?'

'Can't say, for sure. I'm not his keeper, either. Try again after seven this evening, to be on the safe side.'

'Very well. I'll do just that. Thank you so much for your help. You're too kind,' he finished sarcastically, and hung up.

Maddie scowled at the dead receiver, then shuddered. Something told her she'd just made a dangerous enemy. Yet how could that be? Max was in England. There was nothing he could do to her.

She replaced the receiver and slid from the stool, her hand drifting over her very flat stomach in an oddly protective gesture as she made her way carefully down the spiral staircase. Immediately, a warm, squishy feeling flooded through her. She had done the right thing. No matter what happened, Miles's baby would always be hers, to love and care for. A true love-child in every way.

It was five after six. The dinner was in the oven, the table was set with candles and flowers, and Maddie was dressed to kill in a fantastic little black woollen dress with a low scooped neckline, long tight sexy sleeves and an outrageously short twirly skirt.

In deference to the cooler weather, her long legs were encased in black stockings, then made to look even longer with the highest of black high heels. Her hair was up the way Miles liked it—erotically haphazard, with curls falling around her face and neck. She was wearing the earrings he'd given her, plus a wildly exotic scent he'd once complimented.

Maddie knew she looked sexy. Hell, she *felt* sexy.

She had actually spent the first half of the day quite depressed. But depression did not sit well with Maddie. It was such a futile state of mind.

Finally, her zest for life and sheer commonsense snapped her out of it. She still had two months at least of Miles's company, she reasoned, and she wasn't going to waste a single minute by crying over spilt milk or getting maudlin over a future that hadn't eventuated yet. Who knew? Maybe a miracle would happen, and Miles would find out he couldn't live without her. He certainly would never think that if he came home to find her skulking and sulking around the house like a spoiled child.

She'd made her bed, and damn it all, she was going to enjoy lying in it!

So she'd pulled out all stops and was now impatiently waiting for him to return and appreciate her efforts. He'd rung her from Julian's house five minutes ago, saying they'd just arrived back and Isabel was insisting he have a cup of coffee before driving home. When she'd told him about his brother's call, he scowled, but promised he would be home by seven.

Maddie glanced at the clock again. Only ten past six. She had a fifty minute wait. She checked the dinner, opened the wine, poured herself a glass then wandered out to stand on the balcony and admire the sea view.

Nothing, in her opinion, compared with the Pacific Ocean at night, and under moonlight. The wind had dropped, and the sea was fairly flat, its black surface a perfect mirror for the full moon and the abundance of stars.

It was a night for romance, she thought as she sipped her wine. A night for lovers.

With the press of a button, she slid the glass windows back a few feet and breathed in the fresh night air. But it was too cold to keep it that way, and she was about to shut them again when she heard the sound of a car accelerating up the driveway beneath her.

Miles was early!

Delighted, she zapped the window into place and hurried to greet him at the top of the spiral staircase. When he didn't appear within a minute, she frowned. When the buzzer went on the front doorbell downstairs, her frown deepened.

Had Miles forgotten his key? Impossible. It was on the key ring with his car keys, and he'd had to drive home.

Obviously, it wasn't Miles. Wondering who it was, she walked over to press the button on the internal security system. 'Yes?' she answered warily.

'It's Max MacMillan, Ms Powers. Has Miles come home yet?'

Maddie was floored. Miles's brother was *here*?

Even the Concorde couldn't get him from England to Australia that fast. The penny was quick to drop. He hadn't rung her from England this morning. He'd rung from Syndey. Miles's brother had come to personally talk his errant younger brother into going home.

'No, he's not,' she said, dismay quickly giving way to a defensive sharpness.

'Then may I come in and wait for him?'

'I suppose so,' came her reluctant answer as she pressed the buzzer that released the lock on the door. 'Just come straight up the steps in front of you, then up the spiral staircase on your right to the top level.'

She gulped back her glass of wine as she waited for him, sensing she might need some Dutch courage before this night was out.

Her eyes rounded when the man behind the voice finally materialised at the top of the staircase.

CHAPTER FOURTEEN

MAX wasn't at all like Miles physically. He was shortish and balding, with small blue eyes, a sleazily thin moustache and a cruel mouth with thin lips.

For all his unprepossessing looks, he was dressed superbly in a dark blue suit and oozed a haughty air of superiority as he returned her perfunctory greeting, then strode past her into the living room.

Not a word was said as he stalked around, narrowed eyes darting here and there. Maddie found herself on the end of as many glances as the decor and the view.

'I can well understand why Miles is so enamoured with his life-style out here,' he pronounced at last. 'This is a startlingly seductive home. And you're a startlingly seductive woman,' he added, his beady blue eyes stripping her as they raked her body from top to toe.

Maddie was taken aback by the openly lewd appraisal and wished Miles would hurry. Unfortunately, it was only half past six, and Julian's house was a good twenty minutes' drive away.

'Can I get you a drink while you're waiting?' she offered coolly, totally ignoring his provocative remark.

'What's that you've been drinking?' he answered brusquely, nodding toward her empty glass.

'A Hunter Valley Chardonnay. I doubt you'd have heard of it.'

'I'll try it, nevertheless.'

Maddie walked over to where the bottle was resting in an ice bucket on the dining table. She was dismayed to see that her hands shook slightly as she poured a glass for her visitor and another for herself before turning to face her unwelcome visitor.

'Miles has grown rather partial to Australian wines,' she said evenly as she gave Max his glass.

'And Australian women, I gather,' he drawled, looking her up and down again before taking a sip of the wine. His eyebrows immediately lifted in a type of snooty surprise. 'From what I can see, the dear boy's taste has improved considerably. This wine is excellent, and you, Ms. Powers, make Annabel look positively anaemic. By the way, has Miles told you about Annabel?'

Maddie knew he wanted her to bite, so she didn't, despite her mind racing with curiosity. Who on earth was Annabel?

'Do call me Madeline,' she said with classic composure, and wandered across the room to settle in her favourite chair. When she glanced up, Max's greedy eyes were gobbling up the extra display of leg and thigh that her sitting down produced. She was infinitely glad of her glass of wine. It gave her something to do and somewhere else to look except into that lascivious face.

Max stayed standing, she noted, making no attempt to sit down. Clearly, he liked the advantage of height. Short men were like that, she'd found.

'Annabel can't hold a candle to you in the sensuality department,' he murmured over the rim of his glass. 'There again, a fiancée doesn't have to be sexy. Better, really, that they're not. Sex and marriage don't mix at all.'

All the breath was knocked out of Maddie's body. Annabel was Miles's fiancée?

Dear God...

Her first reaction was disbelief. But then cold, hard reality began to seep into her stunned brain, and she finally accepted the truth of what Max was saying. It was only natural that a wealthy, handsome, successful man like Miles would have someone waiting for him back home. She should be glad Annabel wasn't his wife!

Her disappointment in Miles was still acute, however, and her distress almost overwhelming, but she simply refused to fall apart. Not in front of this man. This *creep*. She would fall apart later.

'Not that Annabel isn't beautiful,' he was saying. 'Believe me, any man would be proud to have her on his arm as his wife. Miles has chosen well.'

'Why are you telling me this?' Maddie asked, struggling to keep her cool and doing a damned good job.

Max cocked a sardonic eyebrow at her. 'Are you saying you don't *mind* that Miles is engaged to another woman while he's sleeping with you?'

Mind! She wanted to strangle him with her bare hands. She wanted to cut off certain parts of his anatomy, not the least his lying, deceiving tongue.

But be damned if she was going to reveal her inner agony to his smarmy brother.

'That was not my question,' she returned with icy control. 'I asked why you're telling me this. What's it to you what your brother does privately, or what I feel about it?'

He eyed her with an odd mixture of contempt and fascination. 'You're a cool one, aren't you? If you're not interested in marrying Miles—and it's pretty obvious you're not—then it must be money you're after. Or other compensations. I can see Miles has already been buying you jewellery. A decorator's salary wouldn't stretch to diamond earrings like the ones you're wearing tonight.'

He walked over and slid one of the dangling earrings into the palm of his left hand, brushing her neck as he did so. Maddie quivered, her eyes flashing to his.

He smiled at her as he bent to inspect the gems. 'Ah, yes,' he said wryly. 'These would have set Miles back a pretty penny, if I'm any judge. And I *am* a good judge, my dear Madeline. I've had cause to buy lots of jewellery for certain ladies of my acquaintance in the past, items just as expensive as these. You see I have very...expensive...tastes.'

Maddie flinched when he dropped the earrings and began trickling the backs of his fingers over her neck. Her skin broke out in goose bumps of revulsion.

'Take your hands off me,' she snapped, shrugging away from his vile touch.

He laughed and walked round behind the chair. The hair on the back of Maddie's neck stood on end when his hands suddenly curled over her shoulders. His fingertips pressed down quite cruelly into her flesh—thick, amazingly strong fingertips.

'Is that what you said to Miles at first?' he asked while he gripped her shoulders. 'How many pieces of jewellery would it take before you let *me* touch you in far more intimate places than this?'

Maddie was speechless with outrage.

'Cat got your tongue, Madeline?' he rasped, his breath hot in her ear. 'Or are you tallying up your worth? What say I make you a proposition? I'll fly you back to London with me first class, set you up in a furnished flat in Mayfair, give you an expense account, buy you a whole new wardrobe of clothes.'

Maddie's smouldering temper finally exploded into action, sending her springing to her feet and whirling to face her tormentor. 'Are you *insane*?' The words burst forth, her voice shaking with fury.

His eyebrows lifted in mild surprise at her outburst. 'Insane? Far from it. Oh, I see. I'm not offering you enough. You must be more ambitious than I thought. Very well, I'll throw in a luxury car and take you to Paris every other weekend. Or Berlin, if you'd prefer. All I ask in return is unlimited access to your incredibly sexy little body. I won't even demand exclusivity. You can have Miles on the side, if you like, though I don't think he should know about me. Miles, believe it or not, has a peculiar sense of honour.'

Those last three words catapulted some cool commonsense into her overheated brain. For Max was so right. Miles *did* have a sense of honour. He would not—*could* not—act as dishonourably as Max had implied.

Maddie wanted to cry with relief. For she knew then that Miles was not engaged—not any more, anyway. As for the diamond earrings...even if they were real diamonds, he'd deliberately let her think they weren't, hadn't he? Why do that, except to protect her feelings, and their relationship, after she'd said she would not accept expensive presents from a man?

Miles might not love her, but his feelings went deeper than desire. He liked and respected her, and he'd never made her feel cheap. Not like Max had.

She glared at this abomination of mankind who stood before her, so smug in his presumption that he could actually buy her. She'd met some vile men in her time, but this was truly the worst example of his kind she had ever seen. How he came to be Miles's brother was beyond her!

'You disgust me, do you know that?' she spat the words at him. 'I would not let you touch me if you were the last man on earth!'

'Here, here! The woman has taste!'

Maddie gasped, her head snapping round to see the man she loved striding towards her across the room.

Suddenly, something inside her broke, and she ran into Miles's arms. He wrapped them tightly around her and she clung to him, her whole body trembling. He stared at her, his dark frown showing surprise at her uncharacteristically fragile state.

'What in hell are you doing here, Max?' he demanded fiercely. 'And what have you been saying to Maddie to upset her so?'

'He . . . he just showed up,' she whispered. 'He said you were engaged to some woman back in England, then he offered to pay me to go back to London with *him*!'

'Did he now?' Miles grated the question out.

'Now, don't go jumping to conclusions, old man,' Max began blustering in a grandiose manner. 'I was only testing the waters, as they say. Seeing exactly what type of female you've been living with. You can't be too careful, you know. You're a wealthy man, and there are plenty of unscrupulous women in the world who would do anything to trap you into marriage. I sincerely hope you're being careful and not leaving contraception to madam here.'

Miles laughed. 'You wouldn't say that if you knew my Maddie. Not that you weren't trying damned hard to get to know her. No, don't spin me any more lies, Max. You haven't changed one bit. You still think you can buy any woman you fancy.'

'I *can* buy any woman I fancy,' Max claimed derisively. 'It's just a matter of finding the right price.'

'God, I pity you, do you know that?'

Max drew himself up as tall as his five foot six would allow. '*You* pity *me*? That has to be a joke, surely. Have you looked at yourself lately? You look like an adolescent drop-out, with your long hair and your scruffy jeans. As for this...creature... you're cohabiting with. You think I would seriously have anything to do with her? A man couldn't hold his head up in society with something like that on his arm. I only came out here because Mother and Annabel begged me to come and talk some sense into you. They want you to come home, Miles. And so do I. You've played out this fantasy long enough.'

'Annabel has no claim on me, and you know it.' Miles ground the words out. 'I broke off our engagement before I left London.'

'Only technically. You told her you only wanted sex with this woman, and you let her keep the ring. That was tantamount to asking her to wait.'

Maddie flinched in Miles's arms, but his hold remained steadfast. 'Don't talk crap, Max. You know nothing about my feelings for Maddie, and neither does Annabel. I let her keep the ring because I didn't want the damned thing back. And I don't want *her* back.

'*You* can have her, if you like. You'd be a good pair. She wouldn't have to sully herself by sleeping with you too often, and you could have all the women on the side you wanted. Annabel specialises in turning a blind eye. Now get the hell out of here. I see my Maddie has my dinner waiting, and I'm damned hungry. And no, don't expect me to ask you to stay. Frankly, I won't care if I never set eyes on you again!'

Max was truly shocked. Or was that panic Maddie spotted in his eyes? 'You mean you're not going to come back to England? To the company? Ever?'

'Nope. And I'm going to ask Mother to come out here and see what she thinks of life in Australia. I've got a feeling she just might like it.'

'But we need you back in London, Miles,' Max practically begged. 'I, er, the company's in a spot of trouble, and I was hoping you would...'

'Bail you out? Hard cheese, Max. You'll have to stand on your own two feet for once. There's no Daddy to prop up your ego any more. And no baby brother to straighten the financial messes you keep getting yourself in. Bye, Max. And give my regards to Annabel. Now there's a business brain for you. Go ask Annabel what to do, and marry her in exchange for her advice. You could do worse.'

Max glared, first at his brother, then at Maddie.

'If you think he's going to marry you—' he sneered '—then think again. MacMillans don't marry little sluts like you.'

Maddie felt Miles's explosive fury through his arms. She grabbed his fist just as it drew back to hit Max.

'No, don't! He's not worth it.'

Miles thought about that, then nodded, his hand relaxing again. 'You're right. He's not.'

Max must have glimpsed the fist coming, too, for he used their brief conversation to dash for the staircase. The sound of a car roaring off down the driveway twenty seconds later had Maddie sighing with relief.

Miles held her at arms' length, his face showing concern. 'You didn't believe Max when he said I was engaged, did you?'

'Not for a moment,' she lied.

'What else did he say about me? I'll bet none of it was good.'

'He...he did say these earrings were real diamonds,' she ventured carefully.

'And?'

'And he suggested they werc payment for services rendered.'

'Did you believe him?'

'Of course not. If that was the case, you wouldn't have told me they were zircons. *Are* they zircons, Miles?'

His sigh carried resignation. 'No, they're real diamonds, all right.'

'And what are they worth?'

'Maddie, you...'

'The truth, Miles!'

'Thirty-five thousand dollars.'

'Oh, my God!' she gasped, clasping her hands over her ears. 'I won't ever dare wear them again.'

'Yes, you will, once you get used to the idea. And if we're speaking the total truth, then I have another confession to make.'

'Good Lord! What?'

'Vaughan warned me never to say this to you, but it's no use. I can't go on pretending. I love you, Maddie, and I want to marry you.'

A huge lump formed in Maddie's throat. 'You...you love me?' she croaked, her hands falling away from her ears. 'And you want to...to marry me?'

'I most surely do. Now don't say no right off the bat. I'll be good to you, Maddie. And I won't try to change you. Hell, why should I? I love you just the way you are. I'm not like the men your mother got mixed up with. I'm solid and secure. And I love you so much I can't bear the thought of life without you. So what do you say? Will you think about it?'

'Yes,' she whispered.

He frowned. 'Yes what? Yes, you'll think about it?'

'No. Yes, I'll marry you.'

'You *will*?'

'Yes.'

'But...but...'

'I love you, too, Miles.'

He looked stunned. 'She loves me...'

'I've loved you for ages.'

'She's loved me for ages.'

'But I thought you didn't love me.'

'She thought I didn't love her.'

'Miles, stop repeating everything I say!'

'Huh?'

Exasperation had Maddie doing the only thing she could to snap him out of it. She kissed him, then pulled him down on the floor on top of her. Everything went pretty quickly after that, with few words being spoken, except for some select swear words. Miles was not used to Maddie wearing pantihose around the house. They were not the easiest items to remove in the throes of passion.

Afterwards, he stared into her flushed face with a look of awe. 'She loves me,' he said again, then, sighing, rolled onto the rug beside her.

'Miles,' she said softly when his heaving breath subsided.

'Mmm?'

'If we're being truthful, then I have a couple of confessions of my own to make.'

He glanced at her with wary eyes. 'What?'

She gulped, wondering how he would take her news. She decided to start with the less worrying confession first. 'As you know, I've had several lovers before you.'

'I do realise that, Maddie. And I don't mind. Truly. I was no virgin myself when I met you.'

'Yes, but I ... um ... You're the first man I've ever really enjoyed sex with, Miles. There again, you're the first man I've ever truly loved. The others were just ... vengeful trophies.'

'Vengeful trophies?'

'Yes. Paybacks for the way such men treated my mother. I liked having them fall in love with me, and then, after they did, I would end the relationship. I'm not proud of what I did, but I don't think I really hurt any of those men. I used to choose the type who only really loved themselves.'

Miles's thoughtful expression changed to one of pure male triumph. 'You've never really enjoyed sleeping with any other man?'

'Never.'

'Fancy that.' His smug smile slowly faded to a wary frown. 'And what was the other confession? You said there were two.'

Butterflies gathered in Maddie's stomach. 'Er, you know that bit when Max said about you being careful with contraception?'

Miles blinked, then propped himself up on one elbow. 'What are you trying to say, Maddie?'

'I, er, I'm not actually on the pill. I did get a script and I did have it filled in, but I, um, I never started taking it.'

She watched for suspicion in his eyes but found only puzzlement. 'Why not?'

'I...I wanted to have a baby,' she blurted. 'I wasn't trying to trap you, Miles. I didn't think you would ever find out. I thought you would go back to England as planned and I would never see you again and I...I wanted some small part of you to love. I wanted our child. Please don't be angry with me, darling, but I think... I think I might already be pregnant.'

'Oh, Maddie,' he said, his eyes filling with love as hers filled with tears. 'That's the bravest, boldest, sweetest thing I have ever heard. But are you sure? About the baby?'

'Pretty sure.' She choked the words out. She'd never been three weeks late with her period before, and her breasts had a funny, tight, tingly feeling. 'You don't mind, do you?'

'Mind? I'm ecstatic! But shouldn't we be a little more careful? I mean, all this rolling around on the floor couldn't possibly be good for you. Here, let

me help you up. You should be sitting down. Or
lying down. I'll serve up the dinner, and you just
rest.'

'Don't be silly, Miles,' she murmured, pulling him
right back down next to her on the rug. 'The baby's
hardly the size of a pea yet. There's no danger at
all. Not now, and for many months to come.'

'That's great to hear.'

'Miles, are you sure you really love me? It's not
just the sex?'

'I really truly love you.'

He kissed her, and she sighed into his lips.

'What do you think we should call him?' Maddie
asked dreamily.

'Him? Why should it be a him and not a her?'

'Well, there was this article I read once about
choosing the sex of your child. It implied that if
you want a girl you should stop having intercourse
a couple of days before the woman ovulates, because the Xs —which are the boys—are not as ten-
acious and long-living as the Ys—which are the
girls. That way, by the time the woman's egg is
ready to be fertilised, only the Ys have enough zest
left to do the job—hence a girl. But if intercourse
occurs right on ovulation or just after, then the
faster, more aggressive Xs win the race to the egg,
hence a boy is born.'

'I find it hard to believe that the boys have more
zest than the girls, but I'll take your word for it if
you say so, Maddie, my love. So what's your conclusion in all this?'

'So the way we've been at it, Miles, I think we're odds on for a boy.'

'You could be right.'

'There again, Carolyn had a girl...'

'Meaning?'

'Miles, Vaughan is simply crazy about Carolyn, and vice versa. She fell pregnant on the first month they were married. Do you honestly think they were practising abstinence at that stage?'

'You could be right. That Vaughan's a sexy man! Right, we'll have to choose a girl's name as well as a boy's. What do you think of Sarah?' He settled back on the rug and linked his arms above his head. 'Or Janelle?'

'Lovely. Sarah Janelle it will be. And for a boy?'

'I've always liked the name Scott for a boy. It's strong and can't be shortened.'

'Oh, yes, I like that. Scott MacMillan is a good name. Well, that was easy, wasn't it? Let's hope having the baby will be just as easy. I'm a wee bit frightened, Miles, now that I've actually gone and gotten myself pregnant.'

He rolled over and touched her gently on the cheek. 'I'll be there with you, my darling, every step of the way.'

'Will you, Miles? Promise? You won't go fainting on me in the delivery room?'

'Never in a million years,' he assured her, loving her all the more for sounding just a little unsure of herself for once. If there was one thing that had always daunted him about this woman, it was her self-confidence. Maddie never seemed afraid of anyone or anything. It was rather nice to feel needed, as well as just wanted.

He took her hand and put it to his lips. 'You can depend on me, my darling. All the days of your life.'

She smiled her relief, and Miles hoped he would be able to live up to his brave words. The trouble was . . . he'd never been at his best in hospitals. And he wasn't at all sure how he would react to his Maddie in pain.

EPILOGUE

'MADDIE, you're supposed to pant during contractions, not swear,' Miles implored by her side. 'Panting is supposed to make it easier.'

Maddie gave him a baleful look. 'Spoken like a true offsider,' she muttered. 'Why don't *you* pant during my next contraction, then? I prefer to swear. *Nothing* is going to make this ghastly process any easier, and *swearing* makes me feel better! Oh, God, here comes another one. Oh, God, oh!'

She gripped his hand with excruciating tightness, and Miles felt himself begin to panic. The doctor said everything was going quite well considering Maddie had refused an epidural block, opting by and large for a natural childbirth. She had had a couple of Pentothal injections, but nothing seemed to be easing her pain at the moment.

'Shall I call the nurse?' he asked when her face twisted in even more agony. 'What about the doctor? He's just next door, delivering another baby. Shall I call him?'

'No. Yes. No. Oh, God, yes! I suddenly want to push, Miles, and I can't stop. I can feel the baby, Miles. Oh, my God, it's coming out!' she wailed.

Miles pressed the buzzer frantically, then screamed for the doctor. But when no one appeared immediately he had no option but to get down there and do something. For a split second, he was petrified, but then a fierce rush of adrenaline brought with it a surreal confidence along with an instinctive knowledge.

'Pant, Maddie, and try not to push too hard,' he advised as though he did this kind of thing every day. 'Yes, that's it. Easy now. The head's out. Now here comes the shoulders.'

Maddie had stopped swearing and was panting madly now. Even so, the rest of the baby was born with a whoosh, and all of a sudden, Miles was standing there with this very slippery infant in his arms. The door to the room was abruptly flung open, and a harassed doctor raced in, followed by a nurse.

'Good God,' the doctor said. 'Sorry. Difficulties next door. Breach birth. Can't stay long. What a fine-looking boy!' His movements were efficient and economical. 'Nurse Jones, you stay here and finish up for me,' he said five minutes later. 'I must get back next door. Don't worry, Mrs. MacMillan, everything's fine and you don't even need stitches. Good work, Mr. MacMillan!' And clapping Miles on the shoulder, he hurried back to the adjoining room.

Miles had never felt so proud or more of a man. He'd come through for Maddie. And for his son.

A sudden wave of dizziness almost undid his triumph, but he simply refused to faint at that point. But he did sit down, on the chair beside Maddie's head, taking up her tired hand and pressing it to his lips.

'Did you hear, my darling? A boy. We have a beautiful little boy.'

She looked at him, tears running down her face. 'That's wonderful,' she choked out. 'And you were wonderful. Simply wonderful.'

Miles puffed up even more with pride. 'I only did what had to be done, Maddie.'

'No, no, you did more. Much more. What a wonderful man I'm married to.'

'Hush, now, you'll give me a swelled head. Ah, here's little Scott, all cleaned up to meet his mummy. Can I take him?' he asked the nurse.

'Certainly, sir. Just keep the rug tight around him.'

He gathered his son into his arms, and his pride increased. He was so perfect. 'Here, darling. Look what a bobby-dazzler of a baby you've produced! Here, you can hold him if you're not too tired.'

'I don't feel too tired for that.' Maddie took her son in her arms and beamed down upon his surprisingly smooth and pale face. He wasn't at all red and wrinkled, like some newborn babies were. 'Oh, Miles, he's so beautiful. And he has your dimple in his chin. See?'

'Yes, I see,' Miles murmured, a thought resurfacing that had been teasing his subconscious for some time.

'Would you like to try to feed him?' the nurse suggested. 'You are going to breastfeed, aren't you?'

'Heavens, yes!' Maddie said. 'Carolyn said it was much easier than the bottle.'

'And much better for the baby, too,' the nurse said. She was about fifty and of the old school, Miles fancied. She helped Maddie sit up a little, propping some pillows behind her.

Miles was fascinated at how quickly his greedy little son latched on to Maddie's breast.

'You both did very well,' the nurse praised afterwards. 'Some mothers have the devil of trouble breastfeeding, but you'll do just fine. Now I'm going to take the baby down to the nursery for a bathe and a sleep, Mr. MacMillan. Is there anyone in the waiting room who might like to have a peek before I pop him in his cot? You need a sleep, too, Mrs. MacMillan. It's been a long day for both mother and child.'

Miles glanced at Maddie, who told him to go and show everyone their son. She *was* a little tired, but doubted she would sleep. A drink would go down well.

They were all there in the waiting room, seated in a long row against the far wall. Maddie's mother, along with her latest lover, who looked like becoming her first husband. His own mother, who'd come out to Australia for the birth of her first grandchild. Vaughan and Carolyn, who was five months pregnant. Julian and Isabel, who was looking as serene and lovely as ever.

They all jumped to their feet as he walked in, their faces expectant.

He teased them for a second then broke into a wide grin. 'It's a boy!'

Everyone burst with smiles, Maddie's still-pretty mother clapping her enthusiasm. The three men shook his hand while the women kissed his cheek, Carolyn whispering, 'My ultrasound this morning said I'm going to have a boy, too,' when it was her turn.

He shook Vaughan's hand again, congratulating him while trying not to smile knowingly over what Maddie had said produced a boy.

'And when are we going to see this boy of yours?' Vaughan asked.

'This way,' Miles directed. 'The nurse is waiting to give everyone a peek before she bathes him properly and puts him to bed.'

Everyone gushed and gammered through the glass wall of the nursery.

'His name is Scott,' Miles announced. 'We'll think of a middle name later.'

'Scott's a bonnie name,' his mother said warmly from his side. 'And he's a bonnie baby. You're a lucky man, Miles.'

'Did you see he had Uncle Bart's dimple?' Miles said, and turned to look straight into his mother's face with a knowing expression on his own.

Her grey eyes rounded.

Miles knew then, knew what he had suspected for quite a while. He wasn't shocked. Or even upset. He was, in fact, relieved. The decadent genes he didn't want to carry would now never be passed on to his own son.

He took his mother's suddenly shaking hands in his. 'It's all right, Mother. It's all right. I understand fully. Just tell me he was a good man.'

She nodded, clearly unable to speak.

'Then I don't need to know any more than that.'

It wasn't till everyone else had left and they were alone that his mother brought the subject up herself.

'I want to tell you about him,' she said quietly.

'I'd like that.'

'He...he was a tennis player. An Australian tennis player, would you believe?'

'Good God.' Miles was amazed but not displeased. Somehow, it was fitting.

'We met at a party. Your father had been extra beastly that day, and I had to go to this party alone. He pretended he was going to his club, but he was with some tart, I knew. At the party, this young man came up and started talking to me. He was so handsome, and so sweet, and so lonely. It was his first time on tour away from home. Both of us drank a bit too much that night and...and, well, I have to take most of the blame. I was older than him, and a married woman to boot, with a young baby. I don't know what came over me. Some sort of jealous rebellious stand, I suppose. I have no real excuse. I wasn't in love with this young man any more than he was with me.

'Afterwards, I was stricken with remorse and fear. I was terrified of your father finding out.'

'But he's not my father,' Miles reminded her.

'Yes, but I didn't know that then. It wasn't till you were born and I saw that dimple in your chin that I knew for sure.'

'Gran knew, too, didn't she? That's why she made up that rubbish about Uncle Bart.'

'Yes. Bart didn't have a dimple at all. She's always hated William, you see. She saw right through him from the start. She left all her money to you because she knew there wasn't a drop of MacMillan blood in your veins. And because she liked you, of course.'

Miles sighed.

'You're not angry with me?'

'Oh, Mother.' He took her hands in his. 'How could I be? I'm only sorry you had such a miserable marriage.'

'I should have left him. But there was Maxwell to think of, and it wasn't as though your real father ever knew you existed. I never saw him again after that one night.'

'So what became of him? Would I know of him? Did he become a famous tennis player?'

'He might have . . . but he was killed. Over thirty years ago now. It was a motorcycle accident. I read about it in the papers. His name was Jason. Jason Phillips.'

Miles didn't recognise the name and felt a momentary sadness that he would never know this man who had fathered him in a moment of passion and loneliness.

'I'm sorry, son,' his mother said softly.

He leant over and gave her a kiss. 'Don't be silly. You only did what you thought was right, by Max and by me.'

'Max is going to marry Annabel, do you know that?'

Miles laughed. 'He's welcome to her.'

His mother smiled. 'You've done much better with Maddie. She's a sweetie, that girl. Do you know she's offered to give me her old house if I come back here to live? Offered to redecorate it for me, as well, though from what I can see it doesn't need redecorating. We drove past it the other day and it looks a darling little house. And right on the beach, too.'

Miles laughed and laughed and laughed.

'I don't see what's so funny!' his mother exclaimed.

'You will. You've only just begun to know my Maddie. Shall we go along and see if she's still awake?'

'You just can't bear to be away from her for more than a few minutes, can you?'

'No. I love her more than life itself.'

Miles was startled when his mother gave him the biggest hug.

'And what's that for?' he asked warily.

'For being you, dear boy,' she said. 'And for Maddie and Scott and everything! I haven't been this happy in years.'

And neither have I, Miles thought as he went into the room and saw his Maddie, no longer in pain but glowing with health and good spirits.

'So there you are!' she said from where she was sitting up in bed, sipping a cup of tea. 'I asked them to bring me a bottle of Chardonnay but they said alcohol was bad for my milk, which I don't believe for a moment. It would make Scott sleep like a top, I reckon. Still, I'll be going home tomorrow. They said that was too soon, but I said what rot. I feel perfectly fine. Besides, you'll be there to help me for a while, won't you, Nanna?'

'Nanna?' Miles's mother repeated weakly.

'Well you don't want to be called Grandma, do you, darling? Not when you look as good as you do. Which reminds me... Miles, don't you think your mother is too young and spry to be without a man? Not that I think you should get married, darling Nanna. You deserve a little fun for a while, from what I've heard. When you come back here to live permanently, I'll have to see who I can fix you up with for some romantic dalliances.'

Miles did the only thing he could think of to shut Maddie up before his mother fainted.

He kissed her.

Little did he know that his mother was thinking what a clever girl Maddie was. And so right. A romantic dalliance or two was just what she needed after years of neglect! She had to return to England, of course, to settle things and go to Max's wedding. But then she would hurry back, to her son, her grandson, his wife and a new life. Frankly, she just couldn't wait.

Maddie sighed under Miles's tender kiss. Who would have believed last February that by the following January she would be a married woman, and a mother, as well! Or that Miles would turn out to be the one man in the world who could show her the value of true caring and commitment.

'Everyone thinks Scott is simply adorable,' Miles said as his mouth lifted.

Maddie smiled. 'In that case, he must have taken after his father.'

Miles felt his heart flip over. 'I love the things you say.'

'And I love *you*, my darling. Kiss me again,' she whispered passionately. 'A real kiss this time.'

He kissed her again. A real kiss, with his mouth and his tongue and every fibre of his being. What else could he do? He was hers to command. He would be hers till the day he died.

But what of it? he thought with a mixture of fond exasperation and excitement. There were a lot worse ways to spend one's life.

HARLEQUIN  PRESENTS®

Don't miss these fun-filled romances that feature
fantastic men who *eventually* make fabulous fathers.
Ready or not...

Watch for:
June 1997—FINN'S TWINS! (#1890)
by Anne McAllister
July 1997—THE DADDY DEAL (#1897)
by Kathleen O'Brien

FROM HERE TO PATERNITY—
men who find their way to fatherhood
by fair means, by foul, or even by default!

Available wherever Harlequin books are sold.

HARLEQUIN ◆ PRESENTS®

Coming soon...

June 1997—Long Night's Loving (#1887)
by Anne Mather

New York Times bestselling author,
with over 60 million books in print

"Pleasure for her readers." —*Romantic Times*

and

July 1997—A Haunting Obsession (#1893)
by Miranda Lee

one of Presents' brightest stars,
with over 10 million books sold worldwide

"Superb storytelling." —*Romantic Times*

Top author treats from Harlequin Presents.
Make this summer the hottest ever!

And the Winner Is...
You!

...when you pick up these great titles
from our new promotion at your
favorite retail outlet this June!

Diana Palmer
The Case of the Mesmerizing Boss

Betty Neels
The Convenient Wife

Annette Broadrick
Irresistible

Emma Darcy
A Wedding to Remember

Rachel Lee
Lost Warriors

Marie Ferrarella
Father Goose

HARLEQUIN® Silhouette®

Look us up on-line at: http://www.romance.net

ATWI397-R

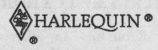